Edmund B. Tuttle

Border Tales

around the camp fire, in the Rocky Mountains

Edmund B. Tuttle

Border Tales
around the camp fire, in the Rocky Mountains

ISBN/EAN: 9783337349363

Printed in Europe, USA, Canada, Australia, Japan

Cover: Foto ©Andreas Hilbeck / pixelio.de

More available books at **www.hansebooks.com**

BORDER TALES

AROUND THE CAMP FIRE, IN THE

ROCKY MOUNTAINS.

BY

CHAPLAIN TUTTLE

(U.S. ARMY),

AUTHOR OF "THE BOY'S BOOK ABOUT INDIANS."

TWO ILLUSTRATIONS BY PHIZ.

NEW YORK:

E. P. DUTTON AND CO.

LONDON:

SAMPSON LOW, MARSTON, SEARLE & RIVINGTON.

1878.

INTRODUCTION.

Boys and girls, as soon as they begin to understand the dangers which surround the early settlers in a new country, are never more diverted than when they can prevail upon some one of the family to read the stories of wild Indian life as told by American travellers. The story of Robinson Crusoe has had more readers, it is thought, than any other adventures, and it has stimulated many a lad to leave a comfortable home in search of the marvellous.

The lives of the Puritans who sailed from England in the *Mayflower*, and landed on the bleak coast of New England, have a lively interest for all English-speaking children, because they found, upon landing at Providence, the whole seacoast swarming with native Indians, who were under the control of a great warrior, named King Philip, of Pokomoket. Besides, there were neighbouring tribes north and west, living as far as New Amsterdam (now New York) and Buffalo, on Lake Erie. The most noted chiefs were Red Jacket, of the Chippeways; Thay-an-da-na-ga, or, as the English named him, John Brandt; Tecumseh, Logan, and others of various tribes.

The writer was born in Auburn, N.Y., in 1815, where the Cayugas once roamed at large on the lake of that name—the Owasco and the Chippeway tribes. Besides, there were other tribes, such as the Onondagas, Senecas, Oneidas, Mohawks, Tuscaroras, which constituted the Iroquois, or Six Nations.

The story begins at the time when the French had possession of nearly all Upper and Lower Canada, and all along the St. Laurence river.

Before entering upon the romantic history of the young people with whom the writer desires to interest his readers, he should here explain his purpose—to preserve, in a connected form, some matters which came under his own observation, after travelling several hundred miles to obtain an interview with such noted chiefs as Red Cloud, Spotted Tail, and Sitting Bull, before the Custer massacre; and to weave in such anecdotes of the experience of himself and others in the U.S. army, as will give a good account of life in America, apart from civilization—just as one may string a necklace with pearls and diamonds, and still not detract from its beauty, but only add variety to the ornament.

> " How came you by this knowledge ?
> By my penny of observation."—*Old Song.*

In the year 1700 the American army was composed of raw militia. No regularly drilled soldiers were to be found on the continent, except such as belonged to the British Government, and these were sent over to garrison forts before the war of the revolution. When the colonies rebelled, and war was declared, the followers of General Washington came from the farms and workshops, mainly to fight against what they believed to be acts of tyranny in imposing heavy taxation. At night these rough and poorly armed soldiers would gather round their camp fires, and while the black servants were cooking the simple fare of salt pork and corn bread, the soldiers passed the time away in relating their experience in felling great forest trees, with which they had built their log cabins ; and how, while cultivating their newly cleared fields for the ripening grain, they had to keep an eye always on bears and wolves prowling along, and to have a loaded rifle at hand to defend themselves. Nor only so; for these hardy pioneers in the forest were subject to attacks from the Indians, who could easily spring out from behind a beech or an oak tree, and plant an arrow or a tomahawk into the white man before he could say "Jack Robinson!"

Who was most to blame in the strife which early began between the first New England settlers and the Indians, there is little doubt. The Indians brought presents to the pale-faces when they landed, of parched corn, wampum, beads, and venison; but they soon found that they were obliged to give up mile after mile of their native lands, to satisfy the greed of men who said they were anxious to make Christians of the poor pagans. How different William Penn acted with the red men on the borders of the Delaware river, we all know. But, then, he was only a Quaker!

Peter Parley has told us, in his histories, how cruel wars were waged upon these simple red men, and how they were slain all along the Providence and Merrimac rivers to the seacoast on Massachusetts Bay, until most of those who remained were at length driven north and west, to the Mohawk river and to the St. Lawrence, and far back into Canada; and it is remarkable that since peace was made between Great Britain and the United States, little or no trouble has arisen to the Canadian Government, while every foot of land the United States have acquired from the Indian tribes, from Massachusetts Bay to the waters westward on Lake Huron, has been stained with the blood of the slain.

In 1789 a treaty was made with the Iroquois, or Six Nations, on the shores of the Cayuga Lake, by which the whites, on certain conditions, should be allowed to cultivate certain lands not included in their "reservation."

An American poet, Mr. P. Hamilton Myers, was requested to write a poem to be read at the centennial celebration in Auburn, in sight of "Logan's Monument," the chief most celebrated in American history:—

> "What of the *red* men, our precursors here?
> Is there no word for them? no pitying tear?
> These were their homes; they trod this very soil.
> Here was their chase, their pastimes, and their toil;
> This their Arcadia, ere the invading foe
> Into their world brought care and ceaseless woe.
> Who mourns for Logan and his vanished race?—
> Auburn, at least, this stigma may efface.

We've built a tower for them, of recent date;
Lo! in our sight, its shafts of sober grey,
High in the air uplifts its granite head;
Its shadow, dial-like, moves o'er our dead."

As the narrative in Part II. contains several incidents of the writer's personal experience, in which a Frenchman, a Dutchman, an African, and a few native-born Americans figure, and, above all, a lovely young lady, together with Indians born on the soil, he will let each tell their stories as well as himself. This is the age of romance, as well as reality; and we are living in times when, never as before, " Men shall run to and fro, and knowledge shall be increased in the earth," as prophesied by Isaiah. Therefore, what the author desires is to bring before the minds of his readers a part of the history of the great State of New York, and to show that the aborigines, or native Indians, have been "more sinned against than sinning."

Now, as to who was killed, who got married and lived many years to tell their children and grandchildren the story here related, time and and a little patience will tell.

It is proper here to mention that all those who figure in the narrative of Part I. had served in the civil war in America for the breaking up of slavery : and the first gun that was fired in the civil war was against Fort Sumpter, South Carolina, in Charleston Harbour, by the Confederates.

Our stories begin really with the surveying party, who were authorized by the Government to find the best route to California. Accordingly, they began their labours at Omaha, on the Missouri river, five hundred miles west of Chicago. The civil engineers, who were to find the best route, had to go through the Indian country, inhabited mostly by the Sioux (pronounced *Soo*) tribe of Indians, the Arapahoes, and Cheyennes. These were hostile to the whites, because they knew that the railroad would frighten and drive away the game ; and if all the buffalo, deer, and antelope were driven off, they must starve and perish.

CONTENTS.

ILLUSTRATIONS.

BORDER TALES

AROUND THE CAMP FIRE, IN THE ROCKY MOUNTAINS.

———◆———

CHAPTER I.

IT would be very interesting were I to describe what is called "an outfit" for a body of travellers across the plains; so much of "hard tack" (biscuit such as one finds on a long sea voyage), coffee, bacon, beans, sugar, condensed milk, and other articles of food, besides camp-kettles, lariats to tether horses and mules, also guns and ammunition, surveying instruments, etc., etc.; but these must be imagined, if never seen, and our story would never be begun if everything had to be described as needed to travel in comfort far away from civilized life.

Our first day's march brought us thirty miles west of the Missouri river, following due west, and quite near the Platte river, which has its origin in the Rocky Mountains, emptying finally into the Missouri at Plattsmouth, Nebraska.

As soon as a halt was ordered, each company of six persons proceeded to open their mess-chest and spread a cloth for supper, the cover serving for a table. Besides, each party of six had a tent and a camp bed, which could be rolled up in the morning and be packed away in the covered waggon, drawn by a mule team. The cooks—two jolly Africans, who were formerly slaves in the South—at once proceeded to build a fire and prepare our evening meal. Both had an eye to their comfort, for they took good care to provide themselves with a bag of corn-meal,* with which to make what they called "a hoe-cake," nicely browned in the ashes. The meal despatched, with generous cups of savoury coffee, all lighted their pipes; and as we sat around the camp fire, I had the honour of telling, or rather of beginning to tell, my first story about prairie-dogs.

* Maize.

CHAPTER II.

WE had traversed a dreary alkaline plain, where scarcely anything grew but wild sagebush and prickly cactus. Here were surely to be found two kinds of animal life, besides the little marmot, new to our experience : sage-hens, as they are called, and plenty of rattlesnakes.

The sage-hens are shot as large as a barnyard cock, and we had promised ourselves a nice meal for mid-day dinner. " The boys," as we always call the soldiers, had bagged a dozen or more. But when we sat down to our roast, we were sadly disappointed. They were so strongly impregnated with sage flavour, that the strongest stomach could not abide them.

As to the snakes, we soon found that they would not harm us if we let them alone. Nature has provided them with rattles on the end of their tails, to warn of danger in meddling with them, and also armed them with a single tooth, containing a small bag of poison at the root of it. In order to protect our horses at night from being bitten, while grazing near camp, they were tied to a stake, with a lariat about fifteen feet in length, made of braided horse-hair, because snakes will not crawl across one or upon a buffalo robe, on which we lay at night.

Here we were close by a regular prairie-dog town, or settlement, as it is called.

PRAIRIE-DOG TOWN.

These animals are so named, not for a resemblance to a dog so much as a squirrel, but because of a habit of barking on appearance of danger. They are yellow in colour, and have a short tail. When surprised, they will scamper off by dozens to their holes, and, sitting up on the top of the little mound which surrounds their earthy dwellings, set up a sharp bark, and then pitch head-foremost into their holes, where it is hard to get at them. They are a species of rodent, and, the soldiers say, make very good eating. So, too, some think of frog's legs, snails, and mule-meat. But as a friend said, "The line must be drawn somewhere;" so we will pass the little dogs and the other articles of food for those who fancy them. One of the Arapahoe chiefs told us that the Indians use the oil tried out from the dogs to cure rheumatism.

These dog towns are a great curiosity in several respects. It was said that rattlesnakes and small owls make their homes underground with the dogs. The dogs dig the holes, and the other two are interlopers. Some doubted the truth of this story, but we proved it. We shot at several of the owls, which alighted on the tops of the little mounds, and down they went into the holes as quickly as possible.

Again, to prove the snake story, a soldier captured a prairie-dog, and placed it in a cage, with some straw to make his nest with. Next morning he found a good-sized rattlesnake coiled up under his pet dog, and both seemed to belong to what Barnum called "the happy family."

Nor were we less fortunate in finding other game. The little gophers abounded in large numbers, being much smaller than the dogs, resembling a chipmuck, with black stripes running along their backs.   The antelopes were plentiful, but very wild, and it required a long-ranged rifle to shoot them at a distance.   Though they are quite as fleet on foot as the deer, they can be imposed upon much easier.   They have an unbounded curiosity, which the Indians take advantage of, and which is thus described:—To draw them within range of their bows and arrows, all they had to do, to impose upon the poor animals, was to tie a white cloth to a pole and wave it to and fro, lying down in the grass, and that at once attracted their notice, so as to induce them to approach within a few rods, and then down they fell, wounded to the death.   The meat is quite tender, rather sweet, and tasting like lamb if young, and like mutton if old.

It was a pretty sight to see them run away, as they followed a trail or path through the tall grass, marching in single file.   We drew a sketch of them one morning, as we came near a drove of antelopes at sunrise.   Some deer were grazing near by, but we had passed on beyond the alkali desert at this time, and had reached water springs, without which we should have famished.

Before the sun had set, we were destined to fall in with some Indians, as well as with some wild buffalo and also grizzly bears.   The Indians were few in number and quite friendly. This we learned by a few signs which all the Indians of the plains understand. As they approach any persons who may be travelling within nearly fifty rods, the headman raises his hand, palm in front, towards the company approaching. This means, " I want to speak with you." If they want to pass by and hold "no talk," then they make a circular motion with one hand, meaning, " I wish to pass by, let me alone." As we met half a dozen Indians, the headman rode forward and put out his hand to us to shake, and uttered the common word of all tribes, "How?" This means, "How do you do?" and is the same as the French salutation, " *Comment vous portez-vous?* " If the Indian is desirous of impressing you with his being very friendly, he says, "How, how?"

But somehow or other the leader did not look very civil. He had a bad eye, and though he had only two of his tribe with him, besides his two squaws, all of whom were mounted on ponies, we kept a sharp look-out on their movements. Without getting off his pony, the one-eyed Indian drew from his bosom a dirty piece of paper in a large envelope, on the corner of which was printed the official stamp of an army quartermaster.   Handing it to us, with a proud look, he said, "Me big heap Indian, heap good!" Opening his credentials with thumb and finger, we read as follows :—

"This Cheyenne Indian wants a pass and recommendation to whites he may meet.   He says he's a good Indian, and never takes any white scalps.   I don't believe a word he says, and do not doubt he's a cussed rascal.   Give him a wide berth !

"JOHN SMITH,

" Quartermaster,

" —— Colorado."

I handed it back to him, and merely remarked it wasn't quite as good as it might be; and giving the old chap some tobacco, and the squaws some beads and a cheap looking-glass, they rode away on their ponies behind the bluffs, much to our satisfaction, as the Indian is an inveterate beggar and won't move on, unless sugar, coffee, flour, and tobacco are given by the pale-faces.

We were destined to meet with a startling adventure toward sunset.   Strict orders were given to prevent the soldiers from separating in a less number than six at a time, and never, on any account, to wander off out of sight of the command and the forage waggons; by no means to fire on any Indians, or waste their ammunition on worthless objects. The sun had just begun to sink behind Laramie Peak as we entered into a gorge, or canyon, and several soldiers had gone ahead, having struck a trail, in the wet sand, of a large bear, which might prove the biggest game they had yet found. Passing out of the canyon, we had to ascend a steep hill in sight of the Rocky Mountains.

Suddenly, a loud, sharp crack of a rifle, then another and another, rang out on the air. Black Pompey, one of the cooks, came running back, with his eyes distended through fear, and yelling at the top of his voice, " Oh, massa, massa! big bear, black as de debbil—old grizzly ! "

We rushed forward, eager to have a shot at his savage highness; but soon we had to halt, as the old fellow, wounded in the shoulder, had turned to give battle, and, bounding with rage, had seized one of the soldiers, and was rolling over and over directly towards the Apaphagie Creek.

What to do we hardly knew at first, for to shoot at the old beast while he was tumbling around would be to endanger the life of the soldier; but a big log stopped their career, and one of the brave boys jumped forward, and with a sharp knife inflicted deadly wounds in the neck of the big animal.

This compelled him to release his hold on the soldier, but not until he had made an ugly wound in the soldier's thigh, and which, we feared, would cripple him for life. He gave a growl, and showing his savage teeth in rage, rolled over and gave up the ghost. He weighed over eight hundred pounds, and measured, from his nose to his tail, nine feet.

We feasted that night on bear meat, all the party having " rump steaks" and plenty of them; and he was so fat that Pompey declared he could make a fortune, if he only had the rich grease that was wasted. He could sell it to the perfumers and barbers in New York city for a dollar a pound.

————

CHAPTER III.

THE first Indian chief I had ever seen in my native town, Auburn, N. Y., was Red Jacket, chief of the Tuscaroras, a tribe of the Algonquins, settled down on a reservation along the shores of Lake Erie, above the Falls of Niagara.

Red Jacket was a noble specimen of his race, and having suffered many wrongs from his white neighbours, would never use the English tongue, but always spoke to the whites through an interpreter. He visited our town one day, and was invited to dine at an hotel. Roast beef, turkey, chicken, and venison were served up at table. Opposite sat a white man, who used some mustard on his beef, and then pushed it over to the two Indians, who had never seen any before. Being an imitative animal, Red Jacket took a good half-teaspoonful with a piece of meat into his mouth, but said nothing as the tears came into his eyes. The other took a little of it, and then asked what made him cry. " Well," said he, " I was thinking of an old Indian who died the other day." Then he asked the other why he cried also. " I was sorry you didn't die when your friend did," was the reply.

I soon found that most of the party had imbibed a prejudice against the Indian race; few having ever seen specimens of them, except such as are found near eastern towns and have become demoralized by imbibing most of the vices and few of the virtues of the whites.

As an illustration of the way Indians were generally treated, I related the following anecdote:—An Indian and a white man concluded to go hunting squirrels, wild turkeys, etc. As night drew on, they had only secured one turkey and a buzzard. As they sat on a log in the wood, it was agreed to divide the game. " Now," said the white man, " I'll take the turkey and you take the buzzard; or you take the buzzard and I'll take the turkey." The Indian scratched his pate, and thus remarked, " Seems to me, you no talk turkey to me at all ! "

Logan, a Mingo chief, many have said, " was believed to be a myth." But this is not so. He was, at an early day, a chief of the Cayugas; and when they wandered forth into Virginia, they left behind them a regular fort, on a hill which overlooks the beautiful city of Auburn (where to-day, as I am writing, rest the

remains of Governor William Henry Seward),
and over the Indian graves there we used to
hunt squirrels, chipmucks, wild pigeons, and
quail. The whole circuit of the hill was (and
still is) surmounted with a rampart, thrown up
in a rude but enduring manner, to ward off the
attacks of an enemy. And many a battle must
have been fought there, as I have seen various
implements of warfare used by the rude savages,
such as tomahawks and stone arrow-heads, dug
out of the trenches.

INDIAN TEPE, OR TENT.

There, on the summit, stands a large monument, erected to the memory of Logan, with this
inscription chiselled on its front—

" WHO MOURNS FOR LOGAN ! "

He was the true friend of the white man, for history records this speech of his, made to Lord Dunmore, Governor of Virginia, in 1774 :—

" I appeal to any white man to say if he ever entered Logan's cabin hungry, and he gave him no meat; if ever he came cold and naked, and he gave him no deerskin to cover him and make him warm !

" All the time of the last long and bloody war Logan remained idle in his cabin, advocating peace. Such was my love for the whites, that my countrymen pointed their finger as they passed, and said, ' Logan is the friend of the white man.'

" I had even have thought to have lived with you, but for the injuries of one man.

" Colonel Cresap, last spring, in cold blood and unprovoked, murdered all the relations of Logan, not even sparing my women and children. There runs not a drop of my blood in the veins of any living creature. This called on me for revenge. I have sought it: I have killed many; I have fully glutted my vengeance.

" For my country I rejoice at the beams of peace, but do not harbour a thought that mine is the joy of fear. Logan never felt fear. He will not turn on his heel to save his life. Who is there to mourn for Logan ? Not one."

CHAPTER IV.

NEXT morning, we saw a party of gold-seekers on their way to the Rocky Mountains, following

PRAIRIE SCHOONERS.

their waggons, covered with canvas, and drawn by mule teams. These waggons were called " prairie schooners."

The illustration shows our waggons and the company of soldiers belonging to our surveying party.

The next evening, after a day's journey with these gold-hunters, brought us forty miles from our last encampment, and when we pitched our tents for the night, all joined in singing songs and telling stories; and in order to make our journey more interesting, it was agreed that the lieutenant's story of the "Twin Brothers," in Part II., should be told on alternate nights, and the other evenings should be given to others of the party who had had much experience in life on the plains.

Major Smith, of the —th Dragoons, volunteered to give us what he had seen among the Ute tribe, near Denver, Colorado; and his story was about

THE SCALP-DANCE.

In 18— I was among the first troops sent out to Pike's Peak, which is about fourteen thousand feet above the level of the sea, to protect the miners. It was there I met Colonel Kit Carson, the great Indian scout and fighter, who was living among the Utes and Pi-ute Indians. He invited myself and others to visit a camp of Indians, four

INDIAN WAR-DANCE.

[Page 17.

miles from Denver, to witness a "war-dance," and although to us these barbarous customs seem unaccountable, they had, probably, their origin in the rites and ceremonies of ancient Israel, of which people the Indians believe they are the lineal descendants.

Already preparations had commenced for the grand scalp glorification, one of the redskins having manufactured a drum by stretching a deerskin over the rim of a cheese-box. Three other drums were soon manufactured; a frying-pan, a tin lard-can, and a brass kettle being used for the bodies of the drums. Having covered his face with paint, the fellow with the tin drum lay down in his tent and commenced practising the weird music of the scalp-dance. He was soon joined by others, when the scalps taken from the Sioux were brought to the front of the tent, and poles to which they were attached stuck in the ground, while the scalps swayed to and fro in the breeze. One by one the braves gathered around, decorated with their best trappings, covered with beads, and painted with red, yellow, green, brown, and white. About an hour before sundown, and before many chiefs had returned from Denver, the scalp-poles were pulled up, and the dusky warriors selected a portion of the prairie remote from any wigwam, where they again fixed the poles about four feet from each other. Then they sat down in a line on the ground, with their backs to the setting sun and their faces to the blood-stained swaying scalps, and commenced a strange chant, beating time upon the drums with sticks, which had for heads, leaves secured to one end with pliant twigs. About half an hour they thus sat chanting, when the squaws began to collect, equally as extravagantly attired and painted.

About thirty had gathered around, when the squaw of the brave who had killed one of the Sioux stepped in front, took one of the scalp-poles, and commenced to march in a circle in front of the musicians, adding at the same time the shrillness of her voice to make the din unearthly. One by one the squaws fell in behind the scalp-bearer, until about a dozen were making the magic circle.

Then up comes another squaw and takes another pole, and starts a procession, moving in a reverse direction to that taken by the first. Upon the arrival of Washington, one of the chiefs, who seemed to know just how the thing should be done, three of the oldest squaws in the tribe formed a third procession, moving inside

the others, and in the same direction as the outside circle. And now drops into line with the
outside circle the third scalp-bearer and the
followers. Korakantie, seemingly the oldest
chief in the collection, advances in front of the
braves—who rose to their feet upon the advent
of the women—and proceeds to dance. A crier
also advances to the front, and commences to
harangue the braves.

On the open prairie, just as the sun is sinking
behind the mountains, half a hundred Indian
warriors, with faces rendered savagely fierce with
paint, and garments of flaming colours, are standing in a line which sways to and fro in time to
beating of drums and the change in tone of the
fiendish music of the scalp-chant. In front of
these the veteran grey-haired warrior of the
tribe dances with strange antics, and the stalwart
form of a huge brave is bent in all conceivable
shapes, as he in loud and excited words recounts
the circumstances of the capture and exhorts the
men. In front of all, the magic circles of squaws
move round, the scalps streaming above their
heads, being beaten in the dust with revengeful
fury or held in their teeth, when the savage grin
is most intense and the chant most uproarious.
Their march is of a limping nature, each proces-

sion giving way with the same leg, in strange unison to the swaying of the braves. These things, together with the weird music only known among savages, when at regular intervals the shrill voices of the women rise above those of the men, and occasionally the startling war-whoop rings loud over all, render the scene one never to be forgotten.

About fifteen hundred persons must have visited the camp and witnessed the scalp-dance, which continued for many hours, and to which Washington, in the name of the tribe, welcomed all white folks, "both braves and squaws," as he expressed it.

CHAPTER V.

THE next morning, at four o'clock, the bugle call sounded a *réveille* just as the big cart-wheel of bright sun was climbing up the bluffs which surrounded our encampment. Exchanging hearty greetings with our " Pike's Peckers," as they called themselves, and wishing them all good luck, they were soon out of sight journeying to the gold and silver mines of Colorado. The day passed with us with little of incident, except those which always attend travellers in shooting game along the Platte river. We came in sight of old Phil Kearney Fort, where we concluded to pass the night. As the fort was abandoned, the only object of interest was the grave, which had a monument in honour of the brave Indians who fell there in a celebrated Indian fight.

CHAPTER VI.

JULESBURG, A FRENCH SETTLEMENT.

ON our arriving next morning at Julesburg ranche, a place owned by an old Frenchman named Jules, and where the stage-horses were always changed on the overland express to California, we met a party of returning miners from Montana, having large leathern belts and sacks containing from five to twenty thousand dollars; one or two having dug out larger quantities of the dust, but of which they did not boast, as it is not safe to let every one know how much valuable property one has in hand in a wild country.

As they carried large navy revolvers and had big knives stuck in their belts, it was easy to be seen they meant to protect themselves from robbers. At night they laid their sacks down for a pillow, while a couple of warm blankets and a wolf's skin sufficed for a bed on the floor. Among the passengers whom we met and spent an evening with, was a Dr. Ben Miller, of Chicago, who had served in the civil war as a surgeon in the 14th Indiana Battery. His experience was mostly in Kansas. To him the writer is indebted for the following anecdote :—

A SOLDIER BOY OF THE 14TH INDIANA BATTERY.

When the war broke out between the North and the South (*first begun in the South*, at Fort Sumpter, South Carolina, where the Secessionists fired upon the American flag), it was found that the regular army was too small to put down the rebellion. President Lincoln issued a proclamation calling for several thousand volunteers. In the State of Indiana a battery was recruited, and a boy named Tommy O'Reilley was enlisted as a drummer-boy, or in some other capacity— "stable-boy," perhaps. However it was, he was ambitious to become a soldier, and he soon showed his smartness in various ways, attracting the captain's attention; and he was intrusted with riding horseback on the leader of the advanced battery of several guns called "six-pounders." Now, this is always a most responsible situation; for when an attack is made upon the enemy, a wrong move in one direction or another in a charge, may bring disaster upon the whole command.

One day a severe fight was begun at Cedar Creek, and the little fellow left his horse (the leader) in charge of a soldier, while he ran forth to carry some shells from the caisson to the guns, which were bellowing out fire and smoke at the enemy. Presently, a shell from the other side burst upon the Union ranks, near the gun which little Tommy served, and it knocked little Tommy's horse down. Dropping his shells, he ran to the poor horse just at the moment the animal fell dead and expired without a groan.

Poor boy! He burst into tears, and cried out, "Oh, my poor horse! Captain, captain, they have killed my poor horse!" Then, suddenly throwing his arms around the horse's neck and kissing him, he sobbed as if his heart would break, saying, "Poor Tom! poor Tom! they have killed my horse!"

He had seen soldier after soldier slain in the battle-field, but he remained unmoved until his horse—poor horse, for whom he had such affection, as for a pet child—was struck down and died before his eyes!

Those who heard the doctor's story could not refrain from tears at this recital of the little soldier boy's sorrow for the pet horse he would ride no more.

CHAPTER VII.

A FEW MORE STORIES BY THE CAMP FIRE ON THE PLATTE RIVER.

OUR chief engineer, before we had settled down to our pipes and tobacco and savoury tin cups of coffee, begged to relate a discovery he had made once near Denver, in Colorado. He had made a halt for dinner one day, and saw two springs of water bubbling up, side by side. He mixed his coffee in the pot from the first, a clear and cool one, and then turned to the other, a hot spring, distant only three or four feet, and put the pot in to boil, without any fire whatever. This is an undoubted fact, and shows how singularly Nature sometimes gives us wonders beyond our experience.

The story of the evening was that of the doctor, or surgeon, of the battery. He witnessed the facts while serving in the army in Kansas, among Kickapoo Indians.

During the War of the Rebellion, the rebels, as well as the northern soldiers, sought to enlist the services of the Indians, although, it is said, the Government did not wish to have the Indians take any part in the strife, knowing the cruelties they always practise on their enemies when captured. But there were Indians engaged on the Confederate side; and if not enlisted in Government service, they would be sure to be employed on the other side.

The doctor's story we may well call—

THE DEAD INDIAN IN AN ARMY WAGGON.

Boys and girls who have seen pictures of Indians, and especially coloured portraits, must have noticed that the warriors always paint their faces in a very hideous manner when about to go upon the war-path. They believe from tradition that if they are slain without any war-paint on

their faces, their spirits will wander to and fro
over the earth, until they find a resting-place in
the bodies of other persons; and this is the
reason why they daub their faces with red ochre,
and then with black stripes running from ear to
ear.   But the whole subject of savages painting
their faces before going to battle, and of some of
them scalping their enemies, is one which is well
worth investigating.   Perhaps Mr. Darwin can
assist us in the matter ?

Now, a regiment of the Plain Indians, or
"blanket Indians," as they are called to distinguish them from civilized Indians, had enlisted
for three months under Colonel Tompkins, and
he had strictly forbidden them to paint their
faces in the usual ugly manner, making them
look like fiends.   But, as they held the above
traditional belief, they evaded the colonel's order,
and, whenever they had a chance to get near a
mud-puddle, would quietly take some of the wet
mud and smear their faces with it.

One day, after a severe fight between the
Kickapoos and General Albert Pike's regiment
of rebel soldiers, the Federals had one of their
Indians wounded during a battle on the re-
publican river.   The Indian was badly wounded,
and on recovering his body it was placed in the

forage waggon, on top of some bags containing "hard tack" (English, biscuit or crackers), and there it was left till nightfall, when a halt was ordered.

But when the Indians began to light their camp fires, they surrounded the commissary waggon to draw their rations. Suddenly a great outcry was heard among them. One of the Indians had discovered that a comrade was dead and lying on the cracker-bags!

Then a regular stampede was made, which, added to howls and shrieks, frightened the commissary nearly to death. A dozen or more rushed off to a mud-hole near by, and began to plaster on the mud as fast as possible, in hopes of averting the sad fate they had incurred by touching a dead Indian with no paint on his face, and none of it on theirs, thus shutting them out of their happy hunting grounds when they should die; and, moreover, they expected the spirit of the dead Indian would take possession of one of them and haunt him all his days on earth.

CHAPTER VIII.

WE continued our journeyings along the Platte as far as Fort Laramie, six hundred miles from Omaha, on the Missouri river, in the Black Hills, and not far from the Powder river country, where the Sioux Indians have their splendid hunting grounds, among the antelopes, the elk, deer, and buffaloes.

Most of the way west of the Missouri river is all level plain, with occasional bluffs, and but one tree for five hundred miles on the Platte river. The survey was over this expanse, running from twenty to thirty miles in width. We were obliged to accept the hospitalities of the officers in camp, and we found among them several who had served all over the country, from the Atlantic to the Pacific, and who, at times, were often absent from civilized life for five long years or more at a time. Sometimès no mail would reach them in two or three months of deep winter snows; and one poor fellow went deranged from leading a pent-up life of monotony and isolation.

One of the officers' wives related a bitter experience of herself, husband, and little ones, in Montana. A continuous snowstorm of a week had piled the snow in banks, in some places twenty feet high, and all egress or ingress was cut off. Food began to grow scarce ; and, alas ! forage for the poor horses and mules, by-and-by, there was none. One night, so desperate had the horses become, they broke loose from the stable, and began gnawing the storm doors in front of the officers' quarters. Next morning, they had to shoot quite a number, to put them out of their misery.

The mule is a queer animal. Thousands are employed in the army transportation of stores. Pack mules, in particular, are indispensable, as thus only can an army transport baggage over high mountains and through gorges where no waggons can pass. The mule is stronger and tougher than a horse, and requires less corn and hay. Sometimes five and often six to ten mules are hitched to an army waggon, and thus as many as ten tons of stores can be hauled thirty miles a day. While journeying across the plains, so keen is their scent, they can sniff the fires of an Indian encampment for more than a mile away, and they begin to snort and show signs of turning away from the road leading to them.

One day some soldiers were sent out to punish some Indians. On ascending the bluff, they discovered the bad fellows down in the valley below, along the side of the Chug water. Fearing the Indians would run away before they could catch them, the soldiers began discharging a mountain howitzer which was strapped on the back of a mule. They had not time to unload it and mount it on wheels. But the charge was too heavy, and the gun kicked, upsetting the mule, and both went rolling and tumbling down the declivity towards the Indians, who ran away for dear life. One Indian was taken prisoner, and they asked him why they ran off without giving battle.

"The big Indian take good heap scalps, and ain't afraid of guns; but when white man load up and fire a whole jackass, we get mighty 'fraid, and run fast as we could!"

The mule-driver is as ingenious in managing his team as the keeper of an elephant is in taming the powerful animal, who could crush his keeper in a moment. But brute force must always give way to superior intelligence. For example, the mule-driver thinks the refractory animal can only be tamed into submission by swearing tremendous oaths at him, and beating him on the head. There is as little reason for such an idea as there is for a captain of a vessel at sea to swear at the sailors in a storm, to enable them to work the ship out of danger. The mule-driver is not always the meekest of men, and passes for a mere cypher when not positively and originally profane. Often, too, there is a sarcasm in his conversation with the poor animals in his charge. But even the modest mule will take a scolding and a bite, rather than go hungry and unrebuked on its toilsome and weary journey. At all hours, when you happen to be in his neighbourhood, you hear the voice of the irritated mule-driver arguing with or cursing his mules.

"You're at it again, are you, curse your heart?" cries the angry driver to a gaunt mule, which is trying to bite a hole in a big sack of corn. "Look here, if you don't leave that there sack alone, I'll take a hammer and knock every darned tooth out of your head! What the deuce do I feed you for?"

Another having a team to manage, breaks out in this jeering style:—"Your name is Humpy Dumpy, and you're a cursed mule. Confound your skin, do you know why you are named Humpy ? " Then cracking his whip at him, says, " Do you know, you're nothing but a mule ? "

Toiling on through a blinding storm, another time you can't avoid hearing a " mule skinner," and you are astonished at his inventions and the singularity of his combinations in the matter of swearing. But these terrible threats and compound, hyphenated " swears " fall unheeded on the weary mule ; and as a final resort the driver appeals to the jaded animal's self-respect, and, with teeth firmly set, cries out, " Git up, Kitty, git up ! Won't you git out of this most inhospitable region of the American continent ? "

Doubtless, there is a good deal of provocation for all this profanity, as men are educated ; but oh ! what a flood of tears a sympathetic recording angel would require to blot out half the records made against the mule-drivers of the Powder river expedition !

One of the officers at Fort Laramie, who had been travelling in California, Texas, and North Mexico, said it had been tried to fire a howitzer on a mule, somewhere on the Rio Grande. The officer, after strapping the little gun on a big mule, invited the colonel and staff to meet him on the bank of the river, just opposite Piedras

Neigras. The charge was one pound of powder and a good-sized cannon ball. After fixing the priming, and attaching a fuse to it, he said, "All is ready." All eyes were intent on seeing how it would work.

The fuze was lighted, and it began to spit and fizzle away just like a Chinese fire-cracker. The mule heard it, and as he was not used to Fourth of July fireworks, got uneasy, as he smelled the burning powder flashing. All at once, he began drawing his forelegs together, and to turn round and round in a circle. This was unlooked for, and if the gun went off, there was no telling which way the shot would go. A panic set in among the officers, and off they rushed pell-mell down the hill, head over heels; while the most timid dropped on the ground, or ran into the chapperell to hide away, if possible, from the dreaded disaster.

When the gun did go off, the poor mule ran frightened to the river, and the last seen of him was that he was swimming the stream and making tracks for some ranche over in Mexico.

D

CHAPTER IX.

SOMETHING MORE ABOUT THE MULE AND WHAT HE CAN DO.

THEY seem to know that their vacation is over; for, even in the confined and crowded corral—a square, strong enclosure or adobe wall and slab fence—it required the best efforts of experienced men and not a little adroit lasso-throwing to reduce to the slavery of the halter animals that, under ordinary circumstances, would come at call and eat bread or salt out of your hand. But after much running and jumping, kicking and snorting, the seventy-two mules were all caught, led down to camp, and tied to a rope fastened by pins close to the ground, where they busied themselves in all sorts of mulish mischief calculated to make the packers swear.

But the circus began when one by one they were led out to have the pack-saddles put on for the first time—first for this season for many, for some the first time in their lives. The pack-saddle in use by the Survey is not the Mexican "sawbuck," which has been generally discarded in

TAMING A MULE.   [Page 35.

the West, but a contrivance introduced from, or
at least through, California, called the *aparejo*.
These pack-saddles are flat bags of firm leather,
joined in the middle and strengthened at the
edges so as to hold their shape perfectly. They
are stuffed moderately full of hay, and when
properly balanced on the mule's back, blankets
having been placed underneath, arch above his
spine and flare out from his sides, the weight of
the load falling equally upon the swelling upper
portion of the ribs, but leaving the ridges of the
backbone untouched. The whole is fastened by
a broad "belly-band," termed a *sinch*, which, by
a method of drawing up loops of rope practised
everywhere through the mountains, known as
sinching, is tightened until a load of three hundred
pounds may be piled high on top and the *aparejo*
not slip an inch from one day's end to the other.
The mule understands very well that it is not
a pleasant thing to have two strong men brace
their feet against his ribs and pull upon a girth
until the contour line of his stomach closely
resembles the outside of Cupid's bow; and sometimes he never does submit, but day after day
and season after season will resist by every
device of obstinacy and agility which a healthy
mule knows how to employ. All soon learn to

swell themselves out when being sinched, and render their muscles so rigid that it is always necessary, after the first mile or so of marching in the morning, to stop and tighten the girths.

FUN FOR THE MULETEERS.

These facts and habits being understood, you can imagine the fun—for those not handling the beasts—likely to ensue from the introduction to it of a green mule, strong in his youth, and fresh from a winter's untrammelled ranging over the prairies. He is led out into an open space, stepping timidly, but, not seeing any cause for alarm, quietly, and before he understands what it all means, he finds that a noose of the lariat about his neck has been slipped over his nose, and discovers that his foes have secured an advantage. He pulls and shakes his head, and stands upright on each end, but all to no avail. The harder he pulls the tighter the noose pinches his nose; so he comes down and stands still. Score one for the packers. Then a man approaches slowly and circumspectly, holding behind him a feather "blind," which he seeks to slip over the mule's head and cover his eyes, so that he shall not see what is being prepared for his delectation. But two long ears stand in the way, and the first touch of the leather is a signal for a jump—for two jumps, indeed; for packers are wise enough in their day and generation to fight shy of the business end of a mule! The next trial is less a matter of caution and more of strength, and here the animal has the advantage and sometimes must be thrown to the ground. It is fine to see the indignation of such a fellow! He falls heavily, yet holds his head high, and essays to rise. But his fore feet are manacled with ropes in the hands of two strong men, and his head is held by a third. Yet he will get up on his hind feet, stand straight up, and dash down with all his weight in futile efforts to get free. Secured with more rope, blinded with leather, allowed only three legs to stand upon, and cursed frightfully, he must submit, though never with good grace.

It is not very often, however, that it is needful to proceed to this extremity, and a mule blinded and held by a firm halter will often allow, without serious resistance, the strange thing to be put upon his back and the straps adjusted—all but one. When that institution called the crupper is to be placed under a young mule's narrative, non-conbatants better leave the coun-

try.   Language fails to express the magnificence
of the kicking!   The light heels describe an arc
from the ground to ten feet above it, and then
strike out at a tangent.   They cut through the
air like whip-lashes, and would penetrate what
they struck like a bullet.   But pretty soon the
mule tires.   Strategy wins, the crupper is gained,
and the first hard pull is made upon the *sinch*,
which holds firmly every hair's breadth gained.
Score another one for the packers, while the
mule springs again and again, with arched back
and head between his forelegs, landing on stiff
legs to jar his burden off, or falling full weight
upon his side and rolling over to scrape it free.
He will stand on his haunches and roll over
backward; he will stand on his head and almost
turn a somersault.   Finally, he will rise up,
shake himself, depress his ears, and stand still
while you tighten the girth and lead him away.
He is conquered.

CHAPTER X.

THE first night after our arrival at Fort Laramie
found us surrounding, not a camp fire, but a comfortable set of quarters.   Major Brent, an old

Indian pioneer from St. Louis, was there. General Harney, the greatest Indian fighter of the early day in the plains, was a visitor also. He was full of anecdote, and at the time over seventy years old; his hair white as snow, and his cheeks red as cherries. His heart was warm toward the red men, who, he said, were the injured party in almost all the quarrels we have had with them. "I never knew," said he, "as a general thing, of any fights in which the white men were not the aggressors." He added, "*I never knew an Indian to break his word.*"

The black boy who cleaned my accoutrements and blacked my boots when near civilization, threw some fresh pine-knots on the fire, and each one of the party having formed a circle round it, our friend the lieutenant went on with his story.

CHAPTER XI.

THE great scarcity of fuel for miles upon miles away from civilization has led California miners and emigrants to devise means of various kinds to enable them to cook their food and boil coffee for breakfast, dinner, and supper. Of course, ham and bacon, or salt pork, fried, with plenty of hard tack, or flour biscuits, made up in a hurry, and quite light with "baking powder" or soda, are the usual stand-by at each meal. Sometimes, indeed quite often, game of some kind is easily found: ducks, sage-hens, wild geese, antelope, or venison.

Now, to cook food, there must be fire. The Mormon emigrants used "buffalo chips" (*i.e.*, the drippings of wild buffalo), and very good fuel it makes. Sage-brush is used, and some freighters and emigrants sling a big log under their waggons, from which to chip off enough to make a fire as they want it.

The encampment for this night was on the Chug water, in sight of "Red Butte" and "Chimney Rock." The appearance a good way off reminds one of a large castle or fortress, and these "*buttes*" are about a hundred feet high, composed of red sandstone.

Our coloured boy had gathered a lot of sage-brush and made a rousing fire to cook the supper, when all hands sat down to watch the movements of the sable cook, whose face was shining in the light of the bright blaze, while he danced about quite lively, to keep the coffee boiling, the bacon frying, and the biscuit from getting scorched.

We were all anxious to have supper ready and despatched as soon as possible, as our appetites were sharp (as all know who visit the plains); and, besides, we had a new story-teller for the evening in the person of "Texas Jack," who had come across the

" STAKE PLAINS "

in Texas, and accidentally. fallen in with us, on his return journey to "the States" from the Sweetwater country and mines. He promised to tell us how elk and black-tailed deer are killed; where he had come from; of the sorrows of the old buck elk; bears, "and their cunning little ways;" and his own views how to settle the "Indian question."

"Well," said he, "what shall I tell you about?"

He was a complete picture of a Western scout, with a tall, sinewy form, bronzed face, flowing locks, and head covered with a Mexican sombrero.

Taking a seat in our midst on a camp chest, and a light for his meerschaum, we asked him to tell us about his late hunt with some charming English fellows, who had come over on pur-

pose to hunt buffalo on the plains, and other
"small deer," such as can be found nowhere else
as in this latitude, and which abound for thousands of miles into and beyond the Rocky
Mountains.

After a few whiffs of his pipe, to see if it was
lighted, he began :—

" Well, there isn't very much to say about that
hunt. You see, Sir John Reid and his cousin,
Mr. Eaton, were about the most sensible men
and best hunters I ever piloted over the plains.
They were

HUNTING FOR TROPHIES

more than anything else, and didn't kill any
game and leave it to rot on the ground. Probably you would like to have me tell you just
how we occupied ourselves during a day, for the
days were pretty much alike, though we were
out about three months, in the Sweetwater
country, Wyoming Territory. There were seven
of us in the party : the two Englishmen, myself,
my assistant hunter—Tom Sun, better known as
' Indian Tom,' a Frenchman, and a

GREAT INDIAN FIGHTER—

a servant for the Englishmen, a waggon-driver,

and a cook. We didn't take much provisions with us, as we killed all our fresh meat. In the morning, I always made it my first business to hustle out Sir John and his cousin. They always seemed in a hurry, but they were always late in getting to the hunt, and liked their blankets in the morning. After breakfast we would get in the ponies—little Indian ponies called *bronchos*, and I tell you they are rascals. I always rode one called Snort, that could kick the hat off your head while you were on his back. Here's a letter I just got from Tom Sun, telling about Robert, the English servant, trying to ride him since I left the plains. Snort threw him three times in as many minutes, and Robert said he was

'A BLOODY BEAT.'

Robert rode in the English style, but found it wouldn't work with mustangs. Well, the game we were after was elk, black-tail deer, antelope, and mountain sheep. The bears were all holed up for the winter, as we started out late in the season. The elk we'd find on the flats, away from the mountains, browsing. Sometimes there would be two or three thousand head in a band, most of them being does and fawns, with a few

bucks scattered around.   In a band of three
thousand head there would not be more than
thirty or forty bucks, for these elk have

MORE WIVES THAN BRIGHAM YOUNG.

When we would sight a band a long way off,
the first thing would be to dispute whether they
were Indians or elk, for the critters, with their
antlers, look at a distance like men on horseback.
We didn't see any Indians, though, all the time
we were out, and I wasn't a bit sorry for that.
After we got near enough to see plainly, we
would look for such antlers as we wanted, and
would go for those.   The best antlers are on the
old, lone bucks, who get driven away from the
bands generally, but sometimes we would find
them in the bands.   Elk are about the

STUPIDEST ANIMALS IN THE WORLD,

and you can get all you want by either sneak-
hunting or stalking.   When they first see you,
they are so silly they will walk right toward
you, but at a shot they start off, always in the
face of the wind, so that they can smell ahead
and see behind.   Their

NATURAL GAIT IS A TROT.

When they are hurried and frightened, they some-times break into a clumsy run, but they can't travel near as fast that way. I have timed elk trotting eight miles in twenty-four minutes, over rough ground. When you get a band started, you charge into them, ride your ponies into the midst of the animals, press aside those you don't want, by pushing their flanks with your hand, and make for those with fine antlers. They never show fight to men, but are the timidest beasts in the world. The only danger you are in is, that your horse might stumble, and then you would be

TRAMPLED TO DEATH BY THEIR SHARP HOOFS.

Often you can ride around a band of them, and as they will stop for the young ones and wounded ones to come up, you can get ahead of them, and take another shot. This was the way our party hunted, for we were after big horns, and not a lot of meat. By sneak-hunting, one man can kill a whole band of elk. He must first get a good stand, in easy range, to leeward of the game, so that he is completely hid, and must kill one with his first shot. They then stand for a short time, with their backs humped up and their hair raised, looking around to see in which direction to run. Finally, the leader will make a break in one direction or another. Now is the important moment. If the hunter makes a good shot, and kills the leader, the whole band are at his mercy. Having made one break, and found danger in that direction, their wits are exhausted, and they just stand huddled together, and one man, if he had ammunition enough, could

KILL A THOUSAND OF THEM.

Black-tail deer are just the same, but white-tail deer will run from the sound of the gun. This style of shooting is called getting a stand on the game. You can get a stand on buffalo, and they will act the same as the elk. I have killed thirty-five buffalo out of a herd in this way, and only stopped because I was tired."

" Hasn't there been some complaint of parties of hunters from abroad slaughtering game needlessly ? "

"Oh yes; but I don't think there has been

much of that sort of thing done lately. I know
our party killed nothing but what they wanted,
and these Englishmen were good shots, and
brought down a buck when they drew a bead on
him. There is a fine of fifty dollars for leaving
any game on the ground. Captain Shaw, an
Englishman who was hunting to the north of
us, did kill forty or fifty old buck elk, which he
left, but that was really a service to the country.
Their meat is no good, and they only worry the
young bucks. You see, these elk are mighty
queer beasts. A buck is

NO ACCOUNT IN THE HERD

after he is three years old ; and the young bucks
have antlers with a single prong, while these big
antlers belong to the old played-out fellows.
These antlers are full grown about September
every year, and are shed every February, and an
old buck has to devote about three-quarters of
the year to getting rid of his old set and putting
on his new. They have pretty bad times over
it. The elk seeks a lonely place, where he can
lie down and reach water by sticking his nose
out, and can get grass without scarcely moving.
Likely he

WON'T STIR A QUARTER OF MILE

during an entire winter. When the new antlers
begin to come, they are very tender at first, with
blood at the points, and covered with a kind of
skin. If he happens to touch them against anything, it hurts like pulling a tooth. So he passes
week after week, with his nose in a stream and
his rump against a rock, doing nothing but nurse
his horns, until it gets to be August, when they
have nearly got their growth. Then some fine
day he takes a scrape on something, and off
comes the covering from his antlers, and then he
sharpens the points on the trees or rocks, and

BEGINS TO FEEL HIS OATS.

He gives himself a big shake, and starts on the
rampage, trumpeting as he goes. About this
time of the year the plains are full of these cries.
I tell you, it's a good thing to kill these old
pestilences, for they are of no use to themselves
or anybody else. It isn't hunters that are making
game scarce out West, by any means. It's the
ignorant emigrants, who

SCARE THE GAME, AND DON'T KILL IT.

These people keep popping away, without hitting anything, and frighten the animals so that they go into country that is strange to them, where they don't know how to find grass and water, and they starve; and that is why so many skeletons bleach in the prairies of the West. Your hunter, if he doesn't want a deer, leaves him, and can kill one without disturbing those grazing in the next canyon; but bunglers manage, without slaughtering much, to drive the game into an unfit country. You see, the elk and the deer and the buffalo can't stand civilization, and are perishing fast; but the antelopes seem to like a little human society, and are increasing in numbers."

"You say that elk are so timid; is that the case with most of the game in the West?"

"Yes, all but the bear. He is the most contrary chap in the world. Elk, buffalo, deer, wolves, you do anything to frighten them, fire a gun, or come upon them suddenly, and they will run away, but a bear

WILL GO FOR YOU.

Old hunters don't want to have any truck with

E

bears. They are always spoiling for a fight, and are so strong and cunning, and swift, and hard to kill, that a man is pretty sure to get the worst of it if he tackles one of then. It was just true what California Joe said, that 'the best place to hunt bears was where there wasn't any.' A grizzly will stand in the middle of the road, growling and getting his mad up, when there isn't a live creature within forty miles of him. If you meet one and turn out for him, he will probably leave you alone; but if you say a word, look out for him. Many a time I have just made some such remark to a bear as, 'Where are you going, Tommy?' when in an instant his arms would be up and ready to tear me to pieces.

"No, sir, we don't go bear-hunting very much, and are willing to cry quits with those fellows. You see, they can run as fast as a horse, and you have to put a bullet into just such a place to kill them, and until they are dead they are dangerous. Tom Sun got treed on a rock by a grizzly once, and the old loafer just waited there at the foot of the rock for twenty-four hours before he made up his mind to walk off. Tom didn't dare shoot, because his rifle was a light one, and he was afraid he might fail to kill the bear, who would then have quietly wiped him off the rock

A BEAR IN A RANCHE. [*Page* 51.

and clawed him to bits. They are the most impudent beggars, and presume on their privileges. Often a big grizzly will walk into camp, as unconcerned as you please, stroll up to a tree where the game is hanging, help himself to what he wants, and go away. Nobody interferes with him. If he is satisfied to go off with the meat, the hunters are satisfied to let him. I have seen a bear walking along, with an entire elk carcase, with the antlers on, weighing as much as eight hundred pounds, tucked under his arm.

A BEAR IN A RANCHE.

" Sometimes one of these fellows visits a ranche when a party is out hunting, and then, I tell you, he makes a mess. They are as mischievous as monkeys, and have no end of curiosity. Likely the first thing he tackles is a cask of syrup. He gets a little of the dripping from the spigot on his paw, tastes it, says, ' That's good,' whacks in the head of the cask, and pulls it over on his head and shoulders, sticking himself all up, but most of the syrup gets into his stomach. Then he finds some tobacco, tastes it, says, ' No good,' and scatters it over the floor. Next comes a sack of flour. He bursts through the cloth with his paw, tastes it, says, 'Pretty good,' but he don't like it much, so he spreads that all around amongst the tobacco, and he adds to the mess blankets, clothes, everything there is in the hut. By-and-by his stomach gets uneasy from too much molasses, and he lies down and takes a roll, and gets himself all plastered over with flour and tobacco. About the time the hunters come home, perhaps, he has got ready to go, and they meet him in the road, the most comical-looking beast you can imagine. He knows he looks queer, but he walks along as much as to say, 'No matter what I look like, I'm a bear, and you had better leave me alone; I've got my belly full of *sorghum,* and don't want any meat, but clear the road for me, or there'll be trouble.' When you get inside, you find there is no comfort there, and likely have to travel fifty miles to get something to eat. He has ransacked everything, and spoiled everything.

LASSOOING A CINNAMON.

"I was once out with a party in Texas, and we came across a big cinnamon bear. We proposed to leave him alone, but there was one fellow, who didn't know as much bear as the rest, who proposed to capture him with his lasso. We told him he had better let out the job, but he was determined; and, sure enough, he made a good throw, and got the loop around the bear's neck. When old Cinnamon felt it get tight, what do you think he did? He just sat up on his haunches, felt of the rope with one paw, and then began pulling it in, hand over hand. There was a horse and a man fast to the other end of the rope, but

THEY HAD TO COME,

both of them. As for the hunter, he jumped off and got away; but the bear drew the pony right up to him, and let his bowels out with one blow of his paw. We killed him afterwards, but that chap never tried lassooing any more cinnamons. No, they're poor hunting, are bears. There are about twenty varieties of them, and the hog-backed grizzly is the worst, but they're all cross."

TEXAS JACK ON THE INDIAN QUESTION.

" How is it about the Indians?"

" Well, they all seem to have gone north, and I reckon are up to the Canada line. We didn't see any Indian signs all the time we were out. You see, the buffalo have all been driven north, and the Indians have to follow them, for they can't be on the war-path without buffalo. They don't like elk, and deer, and small game well enough to live on it, but give them plenty of buffalo meat and they are happy. You know they consider them as their own property. A redskin will speak of buffalo as ' my cattle,' and as long as they can swell around, on horseback, in paint and feathers, and kill one of their cattle whenever they want food, they're all right ; but cut them off from this, and they'll soon come into the agencies, get beef and beans, and be good Indians. The wild Indian and the buffalo are pards, and when one dies the other must. If the Government had put all its soldiers to killing buffalo, instead of trying to kill redskins, and getting butchered themselves, the Indian question would have been settled long ago. As it is, Canada people have been wiser than we. They have fed the Indians, given them blankets and seed corn to plant, regular annuities of money and tobacco, and have sent missionaries among them long before we did ; and the consequence is, they have never had much serious trouble with them."

The bugle call of the 2nd U.S. Cavalry escort sounded just as Texas Jack had concluded his narrative, and we turned into our tents to sleep as sound as roaches, and to rise early with the sun and bid our new friend adieu, as he once more resumed his journey to the city of New York, whither, he and his companions were tending.

CHAPTER XII.

OUR next night's bivouac was far away up in the Yellowstone country. No sooner were our camp fires lighted, than all our party were eager for the stories to begin.

Now, at the expense of being considered tedious and wandering from the subject of our story, I may be permitted to indulge in a short description of this wonderful region where we had encamped. For, next to the Falls of Niagara, the "geysers" are described by Professor Hayden, United States geologist, as "one of the Seven Wonders of the world."

They are located upon the head waters of the Yellowstone river and upper forks of the Missouri river, and comprise portions of the territories of Idaho and Montana.

The wonders of Iceland or New Zealand are dwarfed into nothingness by the stupendous phenomena of "volcanism" (to adopt the language of this noted geologist) which crowd the oasis of the Yellowstone.

He says, "Many of those springs are no longer active, their igneous vents forming shapes the most fantastic, like the 'Dead Chimney' on Gardner's river, the 'Devil's Den,' 'Tower Creek,' formed most likely near the pleiocene period." Elsewhere abound groups and single varieties of true geysers, not less strange and weird-like in form, like the "Mud Cauldron," the "Great Mud Geyser," and the "Giant's Cauldron," *forty feet in diameter*, intermittent in its flow, having been observed by Professor Hayden, and also by General Sherman, to rise and fall eight times in twenty-four. hours, to a range of thirty feet.

In Firehole Valley a vast basin of one hundred and fifty feet in diameter, with a central orifice of twenty-five feet, throws up a mass of water to a height of sixty feet. At a short distance, a series of mud puffs spurt up with a suppressed thud into the air, spreading around their deposits of fine silicious clay, in every hue, from the purest white to a bright rich pink.

Above all, the giant geyser projects volumes of boiling water upwards of two hundred feet in height, the stream mounting a thousand feet or more: the watery pillar sustaining itself unbroken for twenty minutes at a time.

This, a twin geyser of scarcely less grandeur and transcendent feathery column, rivalling in elegance and purity the triumph of Versailles or Sydenham, was measured to rise two hundred and nineteen feet, glittering like a shower of diamonds in the sun.

In the centre of this region, the Yellowstone Lake is described as carrying off the palm of beauty of the whole scenery of the world. The great canyon and lower falls of the Yellowstone river, if less grand than Niagara, would seem to excel those well-known falls in beauty.

The Yosemite itself (pronounced Yo-sem-e-te), the recent pride of the American continent, would seem in many respects here outdone. The great American park will be the object of tourists ere long, as now travellers go to see the Alps in Switzerland.

Now, coming to our story for the night, in full view of this river, we resume our narrative.

Much to our agreeable surprise, a scout, having a Scotch name, but a full-blood Indian of the

tribe called " Warm-Spring Indians," named
Donald McKay, came into our camp from the
Modoc country in Oregon; and he gave us his
experience of Indian traits and character in the
Pacific scope. He had clear views of Indian
superstition, and of the phenomena they claim to
grow out of their belief.

———

CHAPTER XIII.

THE ANIMAL INSTINCT.

SOME one had led Mr. McKay to speak of animal
instinct, and thereby hung several tales that
led by insensible degrees up to what is commonly
called the supernatural.

" I know," said he, " that animals have some
means of communicating ideas to each other, for
I have seen instances of such communication that
I couldn't doubt. A dog, for instance, will talk
with another dog, and has a perfect knowledge
of whatever his master says to him. We were in
an hotel in the east, last week, the proprietor of
which had

A VERY HANDSOME SETTER

that knew as much as some men I have seen. I saw the hotel man tell this animal to go upstairs to a certain room and come down again in a few minutes. The dog went straight where he was told, and while he was gone his master hid a potato in one of the spittoons. When the dog came back, he was told what had been done, and directed to find the potato. There was a wainscoting about the room, with a ledge on the top of it. The first thing Mr. Dog did was to raise himself up and to travel all about the room, nosing that ledge to see if that potato was laid upon it. Then he went to the spittoons and nosed among them until he found what had been hidden."

" Shrewd !" said another,—a theatrical manager, who was present,—" but I saw a sharper thing than that not long ago in Toledo. The manager of the opera-house there has several

VERY FINE IMPORTED BIRD DOGS

that he keeps about the theatre. They got upon the stage one night while the performance was going on, and created a considerable stir. In order that such a thing shouldn't happen again, we took them down the next night and shut them in the box office. That evening, when I came to count up, I found the cash seventeen dollars short. I called the manager down and he tried to straighten out the deficiency. We couldn't make it out at all. It came out just seventeen dollars short every time we counted. At last he happened to notice one of the dogs in the corner, with a sort of sneaking expression in his face. 'I'm hanged,' said he, 'if I don't believe these dogs have got that money.' He went over, and there, sure enough, was a five-dollar note and a two-dollar note wadded up under that dog's paw, and the paw was stretched out so as to cover the bills up from our sight. In another corner sat another dog, looking out of the corners of his eyes, with his nose pointed down, and his tongue running out once in a while in a very quiet way. He went over and found a ten-dollar note under him. Now, what do you suppose inclined those animals to sneak up and steal that money, as they must have done while I wasn't looking ?"

No one offered any theory.

"I'll tell you how the manager explained it. You see, he had been in the habit of taking them with him to market, and giving one or other of them a twenty-five cent scrip to give to the butcher for meat. He believed the dogs knew money when they saw it, and understood that it was good for meat at the market, and that they just cribbed those bills to buy meat with."

This explanation was greeted with a general roar by all but the narrator and Donald McKay, the latter of whom seemed to take it as perfectly reasonable.

ANOTHER DOG STORY.

"I tell you, gentlemen," said he, "I've faith in animal reason. I had a dog, once—or, rather, my father had—that was enough smarter than we to save our lives upon a certain night in the mountains of California. We had been down to Sacramento, my father and I—I was nothing but a boy ; it was in the early times, as long ago as 1850, I think—and my father who was a well-known man in that country, had been entertained by a Mexican gentleman who was very wealthy. They got up a bull and bear fight for him, and there were great times. When we were coming away this Mexican gave my father a great dog, as big as a donkey almost, and very savage. We had a good deal of trouble, I remember, in getting him reconciled to us at all, but after a while he became very much attached to us.

"We went off with a party that my father organized, into the hills to dig for gold. Those were the times when miners felt as though they were throwing their time away for forty or fifty dollars' worth of gold in a day. We wanted five or six hundred or more. The diggings didn't suit us, so my father and I and Bute—that was the dog's name—struck out to prospect a creek about thirty miles off. We were up on the mountains all day, climbing and prospecting around, so that when it came night we were tired enough. We were going to lie down in a nice open place under a tree to sleep, when my father happened to see Indians watching us. We crawled under some brushes about fifty feet, and took Bute in with us and lay down there, and in a few minutes we were both sound asleep.

"I don't know how long we had lain there when I felt my father nudge me. 'Wake up, Donald,' said he, 'there's something crawling through the brush.' Then I felt something, tap—tap—tap, falling across my legs. I tell you, I was scared— I was nothing but a boy then—and I put my hand down and caught hold of the thing that was tapping me. It was Bute's tail. I called father's attention to it, and he said that was what had waked him up. Then we listened, and I could hear a rustling in the brush every minute or two. All at once the dog got up and made a rush in the direction of the rustling. In about half a minute we heard the most awful noise I have ever listened to. It wasn't a bark, nor a growl, nor a roar, but all three together; and then there was a most terrific rumpus. My father said, ' Get up and run.' We didn't wait to see what the trouble was, but we got away from there without loss of time, and ran for about five minutes, when my father stopped himself by throwing his arm around a tree; and we both laid down on the ground. In a little while the dog came back, and I noticed that his head looked black and queer.

"When daylight broke we found out two things that surprised us more than a little. The first was, that if we had run three feet further than the tree we would have run over a sheer precipice of a thousand feet; and the other, that Bute's head was covered with blood. We went back to the place where we were the night before, and some thirty feet from it we found a dead Indian, on his back, with his throat all torn away. The dog knew what the danger was, and first woke us up with his tail and then went and killed the Indian."

This story, and the dramatic manner in which it was told, rather deadened the spirits of the party for a moment, until another member of it related

ANOTHER INSTANCE OF DOG SENSE,

in which a little terrier had frightened a great Newfoundland out of possession of a piece of meat.

"The Indians all believe that animals have spirits," said Mr. McKay. "They certainly have intelligence, and some means of communicating their ideas from one to another. What it is I don't profess to know; but there are Indians what do. That is to say, there are Indians who claim to possess the secret of the language of animals. One old woman of my tribe—the Cayeuse tribe—I know very well, who has done some very strange things in that way. Mind, I don't believe in such things myself, but there is something in it, more than any of us can find out.

"For example, I will tell you of one message this woman brought to me from one of my horses.

I have about five thousand head of horses and cattle, and some of them are of fine breeds. I had one very handsome bay horse that was a runner. You know the Indians are very fond of running races. This horse had beaten everything in all that country, and I had agreed to let him run against a horse that an Indian had brought up from the South somewhere. The day before the race this old woman I speak of came riding along past my place, where the horse was picketed in an enclosure. When she came near, the horse 'nickered' and ran up to the fence, and whinnered for a minute or so. The old woman came to me and said, 'You mustn't let that horse run to-morrow.' I asked her why not. 'Because,' said she, 'he is not in condition to run. He's not well, and he'll be beaten and come out lame.' Well, of course, I paid no attention to that, and the next day the race was run. It came out just as the old woman said. The horse was the worst-beaten horse I ever saw, and he went lame in one of his forelegs for months afterward.

"Well, you might say, 'it happened so.' That was what we said. But there was to be another race shortly afterward, between the horse that beat mine and another. The horse that

F

beat mine was tethered and awaiting for the race when this same old woman came along. He was cavorting and jumping around very uneasily, and any one would have supposed he was full of fire and life. But as soon as she came near he ran up to her and began to nicker. She came to where we were standing, and said to his proprietor, 'That horse says if he runs to-day he will win the race, but he'll die within three days.' The man laughed and paid no attention to her. The race came off, and the next day the horse lay down and died. Now, perhaps some of you gentlemen who read a good deal can explain these things. I can't. There's something in them that I don't pretend to understand.

"There was another old woman in my tribe, with whom I have talked myself, several times, who once died, and was dead three days and came back to life, and told of seeing the

SPIRITS OF ANIMALS IN THE OTHER WORLD

—what we call the happy hunting ground."

"Tell us about it," chimed in three or four.

"Well, I don't know whether you would say she died or not. I believe there are phases of catalepsy that produce trances like that. But there was a strange circumstance connected with the trance that makes it somewhat different from other cases I have heard of among you white men. When a Cayeuse dies, it is a custom to wait until all the relatives see the body before the burial takes place. When this old woman died—or seemed to die—one of her sons was about a hundred miles or so away, and he had to be sent for to come home. It was the third day after when he came; and they were just about to bury the body, when

LIFE CAME BACK AGAIN.

The old woman sat up, and began to sing a song that was strange to the ears of the people. All our Indian songs have meanings; and though they sound all alike to you white men, there is a great difference between them. When an Indian comes to hear one of your violin or piano players, the music seems to him just what our music seems to you—nothing but a bum-bum, any way. Well, this song was very strange; and when the old woman had finished singing it, she explained that she had learned it from the spirits. She said she had really died; and that the first she knew she was lying on the grass in a beautiful country, and the spirits of animals and birds were moving about, and everything was happy and pleasant. Then she wandered about awhile, and came to the spirits of

THE OLD CHIEF, KOOM,

and his warriors. Koom was an old chief that had died a great, great many years before. He had been a tyrant and a wicked man while he was alive, and had a band of followers who were as hard as he. These spirits were black, and they seemed very downhearted and gloomy. There seemed to be a line in that country, and on one side of it everything was beautiful and pleasant, and on the other side everything was barren and ugly. Koom and his warriors were on the bad side. On the other side she saw Towanka and his people, among whom were many that she knew; and they were enjoying themselves and having a good time of it. Towanka was also an old Cayeuse chief, dead many years, who in his life had been

A GOOD AND JUST MAN.

She went over to them, and they told her she had died before her time; that she was not prepared for that happy land, and must go back again for three years to her people. Before they sent her back they taught her this song and told her that her people should sing it at burials, because it would help the spirit of the dead person on its way to the happy hunting grounds. And to this day that song is sung at Indian funerals. I saw her many a time afterward, before she died—and, by the way, she died in just three years from that trance."

"She was what a white spiritualist would call

A TRANCE MEDIUM,

wasn't she?" asked one who had given considerable study to spiritual phenomena.

"I suppose so. I didn't know anything about what you call spiritualism until I came east," replied McKay. "But the same thing has been known and recognized among the Indians, at least of Oregon and Washington, these hundreds of years. We have what we call our medicine men, who practise it. The Indians are great believers in spirits and dreams. I suppose it is natural for men who are alone with nature most of their lives to be superstitious. I have heard that your white sailors become superstitious from being so much in the solitudes of the sea. Why shouldn't the Indians, from being in the solitudes of the mountains and the forests ? A brave lies down to sleep, and wakes up and says, ' To-day I will be killed,' or ' To-day I will kill some one,' or ' To-day such and such a thing will happen to me.' They dream it, and they believe what they dream.

THE MEDICINE MEN

go to sleep, and the spirits of birds or beasts or snakes come and tell them what will happen. Each medicine man has what he calls his great medicine—the spirit of an eagle or a buffalo, or a rattlesnake or some other animal. The rattlesnake is the greatest medicine. It used to be so that a medicine man's life was not safe for a moment. You understand, the people hire them when there is sickness. Suppose you had a sick child, and I am a medicine man, and you call me to see it. I go, and when I have seen it and you pay me, I go away, and the child grows no better—perhaps worse. You call in another medicine man, who has a spite against me. He looks at your child, and says, ' I can't do anything for it ; the other medicine man has a spite against you for something, and he has put his strong medicine in her ' (that is, what your white medicine men call magnetism), 'and mine is not strong enough to overcome it. She will die.' Then, you say nothing, but you go and kill me, and that ends it. Nothing is done to you. So it was that medicine men were not safe. Lately the people have some new religion that I don't understand, but it must be better than the old, for the medicine men are no longer in peril of their lives."

"Do the medicine men have to go through some preparation for their profession ? " some one asked.

" Oh yes, of course. For instance, suppose you were a chief, and you had a son you thought had some fitness for being a medicine man ; you send for the medicine men, and they come and hold a council about it, and find out if the boy has any medicine—— "

" Any familiar spirit ? "

" Yes. And if they find he has, they teach him a little at a time. He has to commence small. His medicine at first is probably some small bird or little animal. Then he gets along farther, until maybe he reaches the owl " (pointing to a large stuffed specimen of the owl kind that stood near), "and when he comes that far, he is wise. If I was a medicine man and understood what that bird knew when it was alive, I would be wise, for I could see farther than other men, and see in the dark, as the owl can. The big poison or

BIG MEDICINE IS THE RATTLESNAKE.

That is the greatest and the wisest of them all. If it is a girl that wishes to become a medicine woman, she is taken when she is thirteen or fourteen, and put in a dark *tepee* and kept there five days. No one can see her. Food is put into the *tepee* for her, and she is left quite alone with the spirits. Then, on the fifth day, the big medicine man goes in and mesmerizes her, and she becomes stiff and hard as a figure of stone, and remains so until the big medicine man releases her. When she comes to again, she has medicine. She is a medicine woman. Sometimes they have

MEDICINE DANCES,

to see who is the greatest. Maybe it is the big medicine men that give it; maybe it is a chief, who says, ' Come, now, let us see who is the most skilful among you.' Whoever it is pays all the expenses and feeds the people while it lasts—probably five days. The Indians come in from great distances. A platform is built on pieces of wood that spring up and down, and over the platform is thrown a buffalo skin. Then the chief or whoever it is that gives the feast says, ' Now, who is the medicine man? Come, let us see.' The medicine men always allow the oldest to go first. He mounts up on the platform, and begins to spring it up and down and sing; and all the people follow his motions with their hands, and sing too. By-and-by his medicine comes, and he speaks wisdom. Then he goes down, and the chief repeats the invitation. Suppose there is some young fellow in the crowd who can do some little tricks, and has some medicine, and he wants to show what he can do, he sings out, ' Well, I can do these things like him;' and he jumps upon the platform and begins to spring it up and down and sing, while the people keep time and sing as before. The older medicine men don't like this. They say among themselves, ' Who is this young fellow that puts himself forward before the medicine men? We will teach him a lesson.' So they close their eyes, and they say they

SEE HIS MEDICINE COMING.

They tell what it is—maybe a buffalo. They tell what divide it is coming down, and what it is like, and when it is coming nearer and nearer, until one cries out, 'Here it is,' and catches at it, and all the medicine men pitch upon it, and throw it down. Then the young fellow cannot have his medicine. They hold it, and he knows they have been too smart for him. He falls down upon the platform, and begs, 'Here, I have so many horses and so many cattle, and so on. Take it all, only let me live.' That is enough. The medicine men have got his property, and they let him go."

"These proceedings are not unlike some that the media go through—I mean in general, not with regard to the fleecing of an aspirant," suggested the spirit student. "And I dare say the white spiritualist would indorse them, so far as they go, with the explanation that as the Indians are controlled by the lower animals, the manifestations are necessarily base and of an inferior order."

"My brother, Dr. McKay, who was educated and practises medicine in a New England city," pursued Mr. McKay, "was out to visit us a year or two ago, and I remember his making a speech to our people, which I interpreted, in which he

CALLED THEM FOOLS

for listening to, much less believing in, such nonsense. We called to see him a few weeks ago, and while we were at his house there came a very nice-looking lady, who said she wanted to see the Indians. We were shown to her; and then she said she was a medium, and that she had received a communication from her controlling spirit, directing her to call upon us and transmit a message. The Indians, when I explained it to them, at once formed about her as they do about their medicine men at home, and began to sing. In a moment she went into a trance, and began to speak in the Indian tongue. I paid little attention to it, for, as I told you, I don't understand such things, and don't like to meddle with them; but the Indians told me that she gave them a message from an old chief who long since passed away. I had a laugh at my brother about it. ' You called us ignorant fools for believing in such things out in the west,' said I, ' and yet when I come east among the enlightened white folks I find them going on just the same.' He hadn't a word to say."

CHAPTER XIV.

A CONTINUATION OF THE SUPERNATURAL.

As an instance of some strange coincidences we cannot explain, with our limited knowledge, we have a remarkable event to narrate in the accident and death of

BISHOP HENRY W. LEE, OF IOWA.

Bishop Lee, well known, and for years the personal friend of the writer, resided in Davenport, Iowa, in 1874. One night in September (we think it was), he rose from his bed to get a glass of water. The room was dark, and he mistook his way into another room, and fell upon the stairs, thereby dislocating one of his wrists, which was very painful, but not supposed alarming. He had, at that time, a son living in Kansas, with his wife. At two o'clock the son awoke out of sleep, and addressed his wife, saying, "I have had a bad dream; something has happened to father." He looked at his watch, and saw it was just two o'clock. This corresponded with the exact time the accident had occurred !

The bishop's physician had been obliged to amputate the hand in the morning, but gangrene set in, and in a few days he died.

CHAPTER XV.

THE next day an order came from the War Department to go into " winter quarters," and the soldiers went to work in building suitable barracks for the officers and themselves, at Fort David Russell, three miles from Cheyenne. But I know my young friends are becoming very anxious to commence the romance in Part II., therefore I will not detain them by enumerating the many difficulties connected with building a " post," sometimes called a fort, far away from civilization. I will merely say that during the long winter evenings, after the barracks were completed, the lieutenant enlivened our stay by telling us the remainder of his story of " The Twin Brothers." I hope my readers may find it as interesting to them as it was to us.

PART II.

---•◦•---

THE TWIN BROTHERS.

A ROMANCE OF THE FOREST.

A Tale of Indian Life among the Cayuga Indians.

> " Owasco's waters sweetly slept,
>   Owasco's banks were bright and green ;
> The willow on her margin wept,
>   The wild-fowl on her wave were seen :
> And nature's golden charms were shed
> As richly round her quiet bed,
> From flowered mead to mountain brow,
> A century since, as they are now ;
> The same pure purple light was flung
>   At morn across the water's breast ;
> The same rich crimson curtains hung
>   At eve around the glowing west."

In 1856, in my youth, I contributed to the *Auburn Miscellany* some of my early productions. The late Mr. Frederick Prince was publisher and printer. It is due to his memory to say that the following story is the joint work of him and myself. It is hoped, in its new dress, that it will lose nothing of the interest which attended its first introduction, especially among my early friends in Western New York.

THE AUTHOR.

THE TWIN BROTHERS.

CHAPTER I.

IT was during the early day, the day-dawn, of American history, that the stirring scenes of our main story begin, when history tells of the fearless march of General Sullivan through New York State, along the Mohawk river to Lake Erie, followed by his band of dauntless continental heroes, traversing the woods and swamps, and fording rivers, meeting with opposition from the Indians, who felt that no white man had the right to trespass on their hunting grounds, or fish in their streams, which the Great Spirit had made for His favourite children, the red men of the forest.

On the 1st of September, 1779, two Dutchmen, born in New Amsterdam (now New York), were standing on the shore of the river Hudson, about half-way between Yonkers and Dobb's Ferry, near a small cluster of log houses.

"Do you see that craft sailing up the river

G

from New Amsterdam ?" said one of them, named
Dick Van Buren, a stalwart-built young man of
nineteen, to his cousin and companion, young
Diedrich Knickerbocker. "There are guilders,
bright and shining, stored away on that craft;"
and, shading his eyes with his hand from the sun,
he took a good look at the cutter, as she tossed
the spray from her prow while beating up against
wind and tide.

"Gold, did you say, cousin Dick ?"

"Yaw, yaw, mein himmel; dere is dat same ting
in heaps, bagsful."

"Maybe too," replied the other.

"I knows it; yes, I knows all about it.—
What *you* say to yonder sail, Mister Le Fort?"
turning to a tall figure with a French aspect,
visible as he approached the two Dutchmen.

"What do I say about that clipper, down in
the turn of the river ?" replied Le Fort.

"Oh, yaw, yaw, I think she's got a precious
cargo," said Van Buren.

"No. She's an American cruiser, a sort of
phantom ship, that never comes and goes, never
lands a cargo. Her skipper always sleeps with
one eye open; knows all the pirates of the sea;
and all the land-sharks also, who swarm here, he
knows better than you or I."

"Well, what do I know, do you think?" said the Dutchman, colouring in the face.

"You know quite enough to enable the king's customs to buy a halter for your neck for 'lifting' some of the plunder from vessels trading here," said Le Fort.

"Now, you stop such insinuations," said the other young fellow, "against Van Buren."

"No, no," said Van Buren; "nor shall you accuse *me* of plunder, when *you* are hand and glove, cahoot, with all the outlaws between the East and North rivers, and on Long Island."

"It's a downright lie; and he who utters such words shall eat them, and sink or float in the stream!" loudly spoke Le Fort, as his angry tones almost choked him with rage, while his eyes flashed defiance to both of them.

"I may eat my own words, but you can't choke me down with yours," said Van Buren, giving his duck trousers a hoist, and twirling a chew of pigtail tobacco in his cheek.

"Then take that to chew first," said Le Fort, as he raised his stalwart arm, and giving Van Buren a blow which was enough to fell an ox.

"And so I spit at you," said Van Buren, as he planted a settler between the eyes of Le Fort.

"You'll swallow yet, or choke," said the latter,

as he recovered himself, and threw his whole weight forward, grappling his adversary by the throat with a power that soon made the complexion of Van Buren turn a dark hue, his eyes to shoot out, and his tongue to come out of his mouth, forced by the tight grip of his enemy.

"Enough! hold!" cried Diedrich. "Oh, mine Got! I'll tear you limb from limb."

Le Fort knew the almost superhuman strength of the lad who spoke, but his French blood was roused, and he still held fast his victim.

"Will you let go?" called out the youth.

"No," replied Le Fort; "I will not."

"Then you'll hold no pipe in one hand this night," answered Diedrich, as he seized the hand still clutching the throat of his cousin, and with a sudden twist, crushed the bones of Le Fort's arm, causing him to loose his hold; when Van Buren, almost strangled, fell down half dead. "See that, you rascal!" said the youth, as with a powerful push he thrust Le Fort from him, and giving another twist on his arm, he let go, and Le Fort suddenly found himself sprawling several feet away. "Didn't I tell you to let go?"

The breathless Van Buren began to recover slowly on the ground, but could not utter a word; while Le Fort, writhing in deep pain, rushed away toward the settlement, vowing inwardly a dire revenge for the insult he had received.

*   *   *   *   *

As soon as Van Buren had renewed his speech, he cursed his foe, and uttered all sorts of epithets against Le Fort.

"Cursed traitor!" exclaimed he, "to turn informer and betray his neighbours! Does he, think you, cousin, imagine that he can put a stop to a Van Buren's trade? Look here, Diedrich" (raising himself up)—"you hear what I say?—that sneaking, praying tell-tale shall die for this."

"No, Hans; you mustn't take from any one what you can't restore. Blood for blood is the law, and we must let him bide his time."

"Ah, yes; but his days are short if he dares to cross my path again. But, Diedrich, look at that craft. As I live, I believe she's making for the shore."

"True enough," replied the other. "But can you see the shining sovereigns, Van Buren?"— as he smiled at his cousin.

"You bet your dollar, I *will* see them"—as he bent his eyes on the skipper, sailing her way along the stream like a duck in the river.

"Honest, of course?" said Diedrich.

"Oh, yaw, yaw," playfully said the other.

"But look! yonder comes Le Fort back again, mit four of his comrades."

"Yes, so it is," muttered the youth, as he pressed his teeth tightly together. "Diedrich, if they mean fight, stand still, and I will meet them, if I die for it!"

Young Van Buren, afraid of nothing, stood eyeing the vessel and the coming party. The long, low, black schooner, so different from any he had ever seen before, puzzled him. But his attention was recalled to Le Fort and his party of four, drawing near.

Slowly Le Fort and his party came toward the bank, while he held his injured arm and hand with the other. Soon they halted a little way off, and began to consult what they would do. But by-and-by they drew near, and Le Fort said, "There they are, and you see they were two upon one. I had a poor show for my life."

Van Buren went forward a few steps to meet them, when Le Fort, becoming almost mad with anger, and excited with pain of his injured limb, seized his long knife from behind, and rushed upon his enemy, bidding the rest to follow.

Le Fort's blow, aimed at Van Buren, was parried

by the latter, and they immediately closed in, the former being thrown to the ground.

"Do you take me for a mad dog, by attacking me in this way ?"

Le Fort's companions hesitated, and gazed upon the stalwart young Dutchman. His eyes flashed fire, but he was cool enough to stop with out further damage. Standing on the defensive, he felt his superior strength to his enemy. Le Fort lay still, stunned by his fall, and Diedrich, on seeing the struggle of Van Buren with Le Fort, rushed forward madly to his aid.

"Stop, Van !" cried the youth. "Leave him to me ; I'll soon finish him if his comrades interfere."

But they did not.

It was at this time that Diedrich espied that the schooner had port-holes, and was armed with long six-pounders. No such vessel cruised the Hudson, and to his surprise he saw, among the large crowd on the deck, one clad in bright red uniform, in his Majesty's service.

Much as they would have been glad to row off from the shore in a boat, to explore the strange craft, they could only stand and gaze with wonder till the night closed in, while the vessel rode safely at anchor in the stream.

At day-dawn the whole neighbourhood had gathered on the bank, watching closely the movements on board; and, strange to say, they soon spied the form of the tall half-breed, Le Fort, talking with the officer, as they paced the deck.

"What do you suppose that means?" asked Diedrich of his cousin.

"I'm sure I can't tell," was the reply.

But very soon a skiff containing a dozen persons, a young lady among them, was seen to push off from the craft, pulling up stream toward the shore, and was soon lost in the bend of the river.

"That chap Le Fort has humbugged us fairly," said Van to Diedrich.

"Oh, yaw, yaw," said he, looking sad and disappointed.

Nothing more passed between them; and before the sun had set, it was seen that Diedrich Knickerbocker had gone off, no one knew whither.

*   *   *   *   *

You remember that Le Fort was left the day before prone to the earth, and after they left him he picked himself up with an effort, and wended his way to his log cabin, which stood quite hid in a beech grove. As soon as it became dark, he set out to find the spot where the vessel rode at anchor. As he came near in a small skiff, he was challenged from on deck by a sentinel— " Who goes there ? " After a few words, he was helped up the side on board, and at once went down into the cabin. The next morning, persons on shore saw him talking eagerly with a crowd on deck.

Toward evening, the boat which had been rowed up the river was seen coming back, with Le Fort and two others. Soon after he landed, the schooner was seen to upheave her anchor and sail away down stream towards Mannahatta.

All sorts of surmises arose on shore after the vessel had gotten out of sight, and their curiosity was heightened more the next day at finding Le Fort missing, as well as Knickerbocker. The reason of the absence of Diedrich could not be guessed, as he was nearly always at home ; while the other was so often away as to excite no suspicion.

Day and week followed each other, but no tidings had come from either. The party of Le Fort, who went up the Hudson in the boat, nobody could learn anything of ; but feeling as though some clue could be had, the settlers made up a hunting party, and went the same way as

they had seen the boat rowed. However, a week's
prowling along the banks as far up as Haver-
straw gave no satisfaction, and they set their
faces toward home again, with lots of game, such
as squirrels, partridges, pigeons, and wild ducks.

SETTLERS ENCAMPED.

Then they went up again on the other side of
the river, to where the Mohawk empties into
the Hudson. But the French and Canadian
Indians were constantly skirmishing, and their

scalps were in danger of being taken. While they are brooding over their disappointment, we must leave them for a while, to pass on to the scene where our story has the most interest—

FORT HILL.

It was just one of those lovely moonlight nights during the Indian summer, when the Indians, while at peace, assemble, with other neighbouring tribes, to play their annual game of ball, just before the corn harvest, that along the shores of the beautiful Owasco Lake, before ever John Hardenberg or William Bostwick had made the first white settlement in the creek which flowed out, and on which the former erected his log hut and built a mill, a party came up to the fort, where Logan's monument now is.

Of these, one was a fine-looking young man, with rather a feminine cast of countenance, but still quite strongly built. His attire was a red coat with navy gilt buttons, trousers of buckskin, and he wore the top-boots such as the Cavaliers had brought to Virginia from Old England. For some reason he moved apart from his companions, and anxiously gazed around in search of something not known to the others. Another stood close by, clad as a sailor, and a coal-black negro also, called Sambo Cæsar, usually "Sam" for short; and when he opened his mouth, which he often did with a broad grin, he displayed a splendid set of white teeth like ivory. Both were devoted to the young officer, whom they called "captain." Another was a soldier, carrying a large sword by his side; while the most noticeable of all was a lovely young girl of nineteen or twenty years, attired in an old-fashioned dress suited to travelling through the forest, and on her head was a fur cap, with a single eagle's feather for a plume.

The guide, who had once been a trapper, was clad in a homespun suit of grey, and for some reason took especial care of the young lady, named Estelle. Besides these, William Bostwick, an early emigrant, came among these adventurers in an hour of danger. A fine English mastiff, with an Indian pony from Mexico, comprised the party.

"Oh," exclaimed Allen, the leader, "see what a rampart we have here. Let us halt awhile, for the redskins or Old Scratch himself couldn't reach us, so long as our powder holds out."

Having taken up a position in the centre of

the fort, they gathered some dry sticks and leaves with which to cook their food.

Sambo was delighted with the situation, and was quite amused at the hickory nuts falling on his thick skull, as the limbs swayed to and fro with the breeze and sent them down, ripe and sweet, to be cracked with his teeth. But soon they heard the growls of wild wolves taking alarm at the fire, and they were not long in fleeing away to a safe abode; for a faggot lighted, especially if it is pine-knot, is a sure protection from an attack of any wild animal, even the largest beasts of the forest. Spite of the master's caution, Sambo seized a burning brand, and ran after a large wolf down the hillside, but could not get near enough to seize his tail. "He run like de debbil," said the darkey.

As they gathered round the fire, the captain deemed it only an act of prudence to reconnoitre before retiring for the night.

———

CHAPTER II.

THE party, having lighted their pitch-pine knots, began to make a circuit of the hill on which the fort stood, but as yet only the cry of the wolves was heard. The old trapper, used to all the sounds of various animals in those regions, was quite sure he heard the cry of a panther (or wild cat), one of the most dangerous animals to encounter. It resembled a loud cry of a cat in distress, or that of a child in such a case. However, they marched on bravely for a while, all contented but the old seaman, who declared that, blast his eyes! he would sooner serve in a hand-to-hand fight on a man-of-war, than tackle a grizzly bear or overhaul a catamount; but if they came in his way, and it was a fair fight, he'd go into it.

"Look sharp there, Allen," cried the strong man who carried the sword, and who was called Bond; "if you are not careful, one of the varmints of cats will pounce down on ye from the limb of a tree."

"Let me alone for sharp," replied Allen the

sailor; and he asked the trapper if it was true that a bear can hug one so tightly as to squeeze the breath out of one's body—sure?

Scarcely had these words passed, when a sullen growl, just above his head, saluted his ears, and looking up, they espied a huge black Bruin, weighing at least six hundred pounds.

" Ah!" said the sailor, "walk up and introduce yourself? Just look at his big paw!"

" He wants to shake hands with some of us," said Bond to the old sailor.

Allen shook his firebrand at him, and at once the bear ran up a tree, and turning round on a large beech limb, gave a tremendous growl. Allen was soon after him, and grabbing the beast by the tail to pull him down—a most hazardous experiment. At this the bear began to climb up higher. " I say, old fellow, how's it up aloft?" Allen held on tightly; but not wishing to get up among the small twigs, where the bear would have the best of it, he let go his hold, and dropped on his back. On picking himself up, he saw the rest had gone on, and he soon felt great pain in one of his legs, for the bear had bitten him just before he fell.

On coming up with the party, Bond, laughing at the sailor's attempted bearback ride, said,

" Well, why did you leave your affectionate friend so suddenly ? "

" Well," replied the other, " we had just scratched an acquaintance which might have led us to too great an intimacy, and so we parted company."

" I reckon massa nebber see a bear afore," said Sam.

" Why not, Sam ? "

" 'Cause he grab him on his stern, *behind the fokesail*, instead of by *the bow*. Yaw, yaw !"

" Well, Sam," said the hero, " I wasn't brought up in the woods to be scared by owls."

" Just you 'splain yourself," said Sam.

" Yes, yes," all said, " Don't be too hard on Sam. He's certainly no coward."

Allen said that Sam had been at one time " chief cook and bottle-washer " for an American officer; and while fighting among the everglades of Florida, and while taking a stroll at night-fall among the pine trees near the camp, he presently heard a call out of the bushes, in these words : " *Who cooks for you ? who cooks for you ?* " Taking off his cap politely, he replied, " I cooks for General Taylor, sare ; nobody cooks for me ! " It was only a big white owl hooting, but Sam always said he believed it was a bogey.

The party had now reached the top of the hill, and climbing over the rampart which had been thrown up, leaving a deep trench surrounding the hill for half a mile in circumference, they entered a clump of trees, and soon began to arrange for a night's rest. The air had grown cool and the dew was falling.

" I am sure," said the captain, " that the Indians could not have built this fort without the aid of some white man; for they always fight dodging behind trees, and it is contrary to my experience to see any earthworks constructed by the red men."

" No," said Allen ; "the whites I have met never could tell me anything about it. Their only weapons are arrowheads of flint and tomahawks. These tomahawks have a hole in the handle, with a hollow at the back, about the size of a large thimble, in which they put tobacco, and serve as pipes for smoking the weed which Sir Walter Raleigh first introduced from America to England."

" It must be very old," said the captain, " and it is plain that various tribes have assembled here to hold their war councils and to smoke the peace-pipe."

The blankets, spread on some dry leaves, in-

H

vited to repose. A tent made of deerskins was the bedroom of Estelle, and a large fire, in front of which were piled some pine-knots and hickory branches, made it quite comfortable.

The others, with one exception, were glad to wrap their blankets and overcoats around them, and soon sunk into a slumber which fatigue always makes sweet and sound. " After labour comes rest."

It was while the moon was brightly shining in the west, and the stars keeping company, that the captain had withdrawn to the edge of the fort, and seemed only intent on viewing the heavens. This awoke the rest of the men, who were easily aroused at anything.

"Your captain," said Bond to Allen, pointing to the captain, " must be setting the watch for the night, or taking an observation off the coast."

"Reckon boss am looking out for pirates," said Sam; " ain't he?"

"You be quiet," said the old sailor, "or I'll stop your grog in the morning."

That was enough to shut up Sam's mouth, for he had seen enough of sailor's life to value a glass of liquor and a plug of tobacco (or pigtail, as he called it), as quite necessary to his happiness.

Bond was puzzled to know what the real

character of the young naval captain could be, and could not shut his eyes, nor indeed his mouth, for that matter, till he had put the query to Allen: "Do tell me, if you know, who he really is?"

"Know him? Why, I know him 'like a book.' Knew him when he was only 'knee-high to a hop-toad,' when he began as a cabin-boy."

"All right, my hearty; but depend on it, there's something mysterious, something in the wind, by the way he's watching."

"By-the-by," said Allen, "don't you wish we were safe at home again? It's now nigh to six years since I have heard a word from any of our folks, and we may be *catawampously* chawed up, as they say in Arkansaw, by some of these wild varmints, one of these days."

"Yes," said Sam. "You had a bear all ter yerself to-night; why didn't you cut off one of his hams for supper?"

"You shut up, blackamoor, or I'll put a hornet's nest in your blanket before morning."

But they got tired of quizzing and joking, and soon they were snoring loud enough to awaken any wild birds that might be roosting in the branches of the trees that overshadowed them.

This scene lay within about two miles of the

Owasco Lake, a lovely sheet of water, thus described by one of our native poets (who has written of " Ensenore," a waterfall emptying into the lake about ten miles above the outlet):—

" One of
The seven fair lakes that lie
Like mirrors 'neath the sky,
Upon the shore of that fair lake,
Whose waters are the clearest, brightest ;
Whose silver surges ever break
Upon her pebbled margin lightest ;
Where dips the lark her sportive wings,
And where the robin-redbreast sings,
And where in many a shaded dell
The viewless echoes love to dwell."

The stillness of the forest was just suited to the captain, for he it was who listened to the gurgling creek, which formed an outlet from the lake, as he paced back and forth, looking out for some definite object.

"Yes," said he to himself, " the spot where Estelle's father was buried is here, or I am deceived. I am sure it must be near this spot."

A deep gorge in some rocks, near a huge chestnut tree, was one of the signs to find out the exact spot, and just as he neared it the moon went down and the stars grew dim, and nothing was bright enough to conduct him any further in his search. Pressing his repeater watch, he found it was past the midnight hour.

Turning his face towards the flickering pine-knots of the camp fire, he retraced his steps ; and throwing some fresh limbs on the fire, he turned down his blanket to rest, just as Sambo, woke out of a sound sleep, started up to see who had come and was about to seize a gun and ward off danger, but, being reassured, turned his woolly head to the fire, and soon fell fast asleep again, dreaming of old life among his companions on the plantation.

CHAPTER III.

THE fort never contained more precious lives in the world, than those few who were resting in peace and quietness that night, perhaps dreaming of home and friends, all fast asleep save the young captain, who could not lose consciousness with the thoughts that came crowding in upon his brain.

"And, by the way," said the lieutenant, stopping in his narrative, " did you ever think of it, that there are human beings knit together in body and soul, which time nor eternity can ever sever ?

" We call it fate, that persons are thrown together, whose interests soon become identical, and yet we cannot tell the reason why.

" For instance, why is this ? A stranger comes into your presence, and at once you feel an antipathy towards him, or you feel yourself involuntarily drawn towards him. There's a destiny, call it what we will, that draws one soul to another in spite of ourselves, either for weal or woe, and over which we can exercise little control as to our own wills. Those who were slumbering in perfect security on Fort Hill were totally unlike in many things, yet there was a something which bound them together. There seemed no common bond or interest which united them, and particularly the navy officer, the old sailor, and Sambo; and the two subordinates always yielded themselves in implicit confidence and obedience to their superior."

The young officer, somehow, hung his head, being quite disheartened, perhaps because he had not found the place where Estelle's father had been buried, or because of the lonely forest surrounding him, as he heard the wolf's bark, and the screech-owl crying out " *Too-hoo! too-hoo!*" The night air was cool and chilly, and he sat with his head leaning on his knees, thinking what next he should do.

The black man, Sam, woke up and diverted his attention. " Ah, massa captain, you lie down and have a good sleep; me stay up and watch all danger."

"No, Sam, you lie down. I am all right. No danger at all; lie down and sleep till morning."

" Massa, you ain't agwine to. Dis child—I'll watch ; you sleep till day breaks."

"Well, Sam, I'll do as you say." He then threw himself down beside the others, and, like an infant, slept away the remaining hours.

*   *   *   *   *

The next morning they were early on the alert, and after their usual morning repast, each one set to work to construct a log hut, to protect them from a rainy spell, which usually set in about the 22nd of September, and was called the equinoctial storm ; and this would also serve as a protection from wild beasts or a surprise by the wily Indians. They had not travelled all the way through an almost trackless desert, through swamps, over morasses, and through huge forests, from the Mohawk river to the Owasco, without learning the dangers which beset travellers from the Atlantic Coast. Wild savages, which beset and dog travellers, when once upon their trail, might give them a sudden surprise; the prowling wolf, wild cats, and beasts of huge size, black as ebony; and, added to their fears, violent thunder-storms, succeeded by a downpour of rain, were always to be looked for, and to come when least expected.

In surveying the surroundings a black mass of leaves was discovered up in the crotch of a cypress tree, and Sambo, who could climb a mast, soon found it contained an eagle's nest, with half a dozen young ones in it. Mistaking the darkey for the mother bird, which had flown away to the outlet to catch a fish for their morning repast, they opened wide their mouths for food; but on Sam's clutching at one, they all scrambled out of their nest and took refuge in one of the branches.

Sam grabbed again, and was lucky to get hold of a leg of the nearest bird, but losing his balance, tumbled with it to the ground. As he fell upon a soft heap of leaves, he was not much hurt, but sprang to his feet and gave chase after the bird, which tried to escape. Soon all parties were drawn to the spot, and they were not long in espying the male bird, a bold eagle, soaring round ready to pounce on the nest-robbers. The moment Sam had again seized his prey, the old one, with tremendous velocity, and claws extended, aimed at the woolly head of the negro.

" You varmint, you, keep off! Debbil take you, let me alone !" and giving the young one a toss upward, the old bird seized it and flew with it back to the nest, leaving Sam's wool untouched, much to his delight. For had he once got his sharp claws in his woolly head, Sam might have had his eyes dug out.

The party also set up a loud shout to scare the old one, but not having a gun at hand could not do the bird any harm. These birds are as desperate over the loss of their young as the bears when bereaved of their whelps ; and as the flesh of the eagle is not desirable for food, it is mere wanton cruelty to capture and kill them.

Sam, in his delight, said he could have killed or captured both at once—" only massa, do ye see, he berry proud of de eagle, 'cause he is the national bird o' freedom, and Gineral Washington he always fight de Britishers under de wings ob his feathers !"

" Well," said the sailor, " guess you're right, Sambo, and I'd sooner have my grog stopped, and live on a single hard-tack biscuit a day, than ruffle a quill of his wings or tail. Besides, Sam, the captain has been looking and watching the old bald-head ever so long. See, he's going to climb himself up to the nest."

Such, indeed, was the case. The old bird had flown suddenly away, after assisting his burden; and if birds can talk to each other, as some naturalists suppose, maybe he'd gone to tell the mother to leave off fishing, and come home to watch over her brood in danger.

A DISCOVERY.

However, no sooner did the captain see the way was clear of danger, than he sprang from limb to limb till he reached the nest.

Both Allen and Sam were eagerly watching his movements, when they espied him catch at something above the nest, and as there were no eggs in it, they were astonished to see him grasp a handful of some dark substance and thrust it into his bosom.

"I shouldn't wonder," said Sam, "if he hasn't found the—the treasure, should you?"

"Heaven grant it may be so," said Allen.

But the captain, losing his hold upon a limb—

probably excited—soon interrupted the confab by tumbling down to the spot whereon Sambo had previously fallen. Both scrambled to assist the captain; but Sam, tumbling headlong over a log, fell prone to the earth himself, and, striking a sharp substance with his hand, blood flowed from one of his fingers. On clearing away the leaves, he discovered a regular Indian tomahawk. The cut was not very deep; and on his master's coming up, Sam showed his trophy and his bleeding hand, and said he must have been struck by a dead Indian. Some plaster was applied to his wound, and he hobbled back with his master, to resume work on the log cabin.

CHAPTER IV.

THE ROMANCE OF FORT HILL.

OUR party having travelled all the way from the Hudson river, along the Mohawk, to the outlet of the Owasco without much danger, were not undiscovered by the wily savages from the Onondaga Hills. Luckily for them, they had, in a week's time, constructed a good-sized log cabin, in which they were safe from the pelting rain; and should they be compelled to winter there, in search of a curious and important object, dear as life, they would be in no danger of perishing of cold, nor frozen to death in the heavy banks of snow which covered all the hills and the valleys beneath. Besides, it served as a secure fort in case of danger—an attack by foes —for the old fort was but a kind of breastwork thrown up by digging a trench all round the crest of the hill. Here they had arranged things quite comfortably, spending their days each as they pleased.

The captain kept apart, pursuing his search from morning till night, after he had found the *clue* over the eagle's nest, but kept his secret all to himself. Sambo and Allen went out foraging for game, such as wild pigeons, raccoons, opossums, black and grey squirrels, wild geese, and turkeys; or they would fish in the outlet, in which trout, perch, and bull-heads in great quantities were found, without going as far as the lake from which the fish came.

The powder and shot was running short, and as supplies were only to be obtained at Fort Stanwix, many miles to the east, on the Mohawk, the captain bade them not to waste their powder and lead on animals not needed for food on the table. Not that they had *a table*,—only a couple of chest-lids which stood in place of one, and a sail-cloth was used for a table-cloth. This was not so bad a shift as the poor sometimes resort to, according to Doctor Johnson, who wrote—

" The sheets contrived a double debt to pay—
To serve the bed by night, a tablecloth by day."

The caution to be saving of ball and powder was a timely one, for at nightfall, as Sam was coming along, sauntering near a marsh in search of wild-goose eggs, mud turtles, etc., he heard the cry of a child, as it sounded to his ears. Following through the flags and jumping from one bog to another, scaring owls and kicking mud turtles out of the way in the tamarack swamp, when he heard this cry of a child in such a strange place, as if the child was in great distress, he soon came to a dead halt. But he got his eyes opened ; for right over his head was a wild cat, or panther, several feet long, lying on its belly along a large limb of a tree, ready to spring on its prey ! Sam had never seen one before, but he had heard enough of its fearful power to frighten him almost out of his wits. Turning deadly pale, he started back and ran for dear life to the cabin, scarcely taking breath till he got within the door, when he immediately fell down from fright and exhaustion. All flocked around the poor darkey and begged to know what was the matter.

As soon as the poor fellow could gather speech, his eyes almost out of his head, he exclaimed, "Bear! bear, massa!"

Of course, after a while he recovered his senses, and related how he had nearly sacrificed his life in a benevolent desire to succour a child in distress.

Walker could not resist the opportunity of having a little fun out of the darkey, since all danger was now over. So he asked Sam if he didn't see a polecat, instead of a wild cat.

"Polecat? Not much. You bet your life dat cat eat you all up, sure as you live, if get hold of your skin."

"Yes, Sam; but you said it was a bear when you got safe home. Seems to me you lacked courage on that occasion?"

"Courage! I'se as bold as a lion, when I sees the varmint on the same footing as myself. If I had one of de old continental muskets, such as we had at de battle ob Yorktown, I'd gin him fits! You tink, 'cause I'se whipped by an animal, I'se a coward ?"

"Looks like it," said Walker. "But what do you know about Yorktown, where General Washington won the day over General Cornwallis ?"

"Cornwallis? I guess I knows a heap. He was General Cornwallis, in course, but he ain't now."

"Why not, Sam ?"

"Well, d'ye see, General Washington he smart old man, and he licked Cornwallis on dat occasion, and so now we call him COBWALLIS,— he, he !"

"What for ?"

"'Cause General Washington *shell all de corn* off him too slick. Ha, ha! ho, ho! he, he !"

The other said, "We needn't boast too much. The Britishers made *us* run a good many times, and you must remember our fathers were Englishmen, descendants of a bold race who, with us, can conquer the world !"

"Dat am a fact, massa, but black folks must help 'um."

"Well," said Walker, "all bad feeling between us and the British is now laid aside, and we see how foolish it was in England not to have avoided a quarrel which never should have been begun."

Next morning, Walker, who had been early in the forest, assembled all hands to hear what the captain had to say, as they two were about to go on an excursion to find out something of importance, and they had to give orders for protecting the young lady, Estelle, while they were absent.

The captain called Allen aside from the others, and took from his pocket-book a relic which he had found up in the tree, much to the delight of the other, who exclaimed—

" My eyes, are you not lucky ? "

Had the captain found a gold or silver mine instead, it could not have caused so much joy as this. For were they not out on a search which might cost them all their lives, in order to find out where, dead or alive, was the—— Well, we must not spoil our story of love and fortune just now, by revealing what they came for. It is enough to say that it was long before Walker, with the captain and Sambo, left the fort, branching off through the beech-woods north towards the Lake Ontario.

" A safe and pleasant journey for all of you," said Allen; " and mind you don't stray into any more swamps after mudlarks again, Sam, but march behind the others in regular Indian file."

" Nebber you care for dis darkey, I'm as bold as a lion, and so we'll have a song before we go.

> ' De Lord He lub good nigger well ;
> He know de nigger by de smell ;
> And when de little nigger cry,
> De Lord He gib him 'possum-pie.' "

After a hearty laugh, Allen sat down on a log before the cabin door as soon as the party were out of sight, and soon appeared lost in thought ; while Bond sat within the cabin singing an old revolutionary song, called "The Hunters of Kentucky." One verse will show the nature of the refrain—

> " Ye gentlemen and ladies fair, who grace this famous city,
> Just listen, if you've time to spare, while I rehearse a ditty,
> And for the opportunity conceive yourselves quite lucky,
> For 'tis not often that you see—a hunter from Kentucky !
>   Oh, Kentucky ! the hunters of Kentucky ! "

Estelle spoke up and said, "We three are all there are to protect this fort, I suppose, while the rest are away ? I pray our Heavenly Father that He will guard us from all danger, for it would be dreadful to be set upon by savage Indians, and slaughtered to death in this wilderness ! Some one told me that the Cayuga tribe had made a treaty with the Jesuit missionaries, some time since, on the shores of the Cayuga

I

Lake, eight miles from this, and that we had nothing to fear from them."

"That I can't say," replied Bond; "but of one thing be sure—if we are set upon by Indians, Allen and I will fire the guns, and you can act as 'powder-monkey,' as they say on ship-board, and hand us the ammunition. We'll die in defence of you, and so you needn't lay awake nights, or dream of danger."

"Yes, miss," interrupted the other, "we'll die for you, fighting on our part, if needful; and we are a whole team with our Kentucky rifles."

"I am not afraid of your lack of courage; but what if a hundred bloodthirsty savages attack us at once? How could we offer any resistance, or hold out for any length of time?"

"What would we do? Why, we'd pop 'em over like ninepins; besides, they seldom attack the whites in a log cabin, as they have to fight a concealed foe, and can't imagine what may be their numbers."

"True, they fight their enemies in the open woods, where they can dodge behind the trees to avoid being shot, and the moment a gun is fired at them, they jump out and tomahawk their enemy, if within reach. Did you ever en-counter one in battle?" said Estelle.

" No," replied Bond ; "but I have met a soldier who told me how he outwitted a savage chief in the Florida war, and killed him. He said he had fired away at the Indian from behind a tree for some time, and the Indian cracked away at him. By-and-by, he put his cap on the end of his ramrod and stuck it out, as though he was peeping at the Indian. The savage took aim and shot through the cap, which dropped, but not the soldier. Supposing his enemy had fallen, the chief rushed out to tomahawk him ; but he had made a mistake, and when he drew near, the soldier took aim and shot him dead. He was highly commended by his captain for his strategy."

The day passed off in stillness and quiet, save by the noise of the screaming ravens and the barking of the foxes ; and after the sun went down, the whip-poor-will's shrill cry made it seem more lonely to Estelle, who wondered at the singular kinds of animal life that were found in the forest, of which at home she had never heard before. She wondered, too, at the mystery surrounding the captain's movements, and his search after some tokens he did not explain to her. As the evening shadows thickened, the owls began to screech and hoot, and Estelle, tired and bewildered, threw herself down upon her rude bed, and drew a deerskin over her shoulders, to get some rest. The bold men, after smoking their pipes, agreed to watch by turns till daylight.

Estelle tried in vain to sleep, but images of wild beasts or savage Indians would haunt her, as she fell into a doze now and then. She was sure she heard howlings of wolves close by, and though safe from their attacks, she could not sleep for the terror created in her mind. However, daylight broke in at the window, and the distant rumbling of the Owasco river led her to go out and look upon nature's peaceful scenery, and try to divert her mind from any danger. She soon saw Allen and Bond were on a rise of ground near by, engaged in skinning some squirrels for breakfast.

Passing by them, she ran down the hill, chasing the little chipmucks that crossed her path, until she had wandered quite a distance from the log cabin on the hill.

————

_ CHAPTER V.

WHAT ESTELLE FOUND BY EXPERIENCE AND NOT BY READING.

WE left the young lady heroine of our story on Fort Hill, going from the cabin towards the Owasco river. She had plenty of time to meditate, and so she thought nothing was more likely to inspire awe and dread in one's mind, than to find one's self all alone in a dense forest.

To be cast out in an open boat at sea, with nothing to fix the eye upon but a vast expanse blue above and blue or green below, is awe-inspiring indeed, and one can thus imagine some-what of Estelle's feelings when we left her that morning rambling down the sides of Fort Hill. The men who cut down the large trees with which to build a cabin could tell how old the trees were, by counting the rings which circle round on the top of the stumps. For each year of its growth, a ring is added to its age. Thus, they counted on a huge chestnut fifty rings, show-ing it was fifty years since it was a little sapling ;

and they wondered if so great a change would take place in that romantic and beautiful forest, when emigration from the Old World should come hither and clear the forest to make peaceful homes for millions of our race ?

Suddenly Estelle came to a steep bank of the Owasco creek, and could go no further. Here, plucking some ripe mandrakes to regale her appetite, and sitting down upon a rock, she mused of home and friends far away on the banks of the Hudson. She wept unconsciously at the thought of her isolation from loved ones, and the probable prospect that she might never see them again.

The thought of the village church and the Sunday worship there, as on each Lord's day she had gone to the House of God to worship with loved ones, was naturally tender, and full of regret that all these were lost to her. And though she had brought her Prayer-book with her, and perused it daily (as well on Sundays), still it was a privation ; and she wished, if it were possible, she might be transported, if only for a short time, to wander in the village churchyard, and read once more the tombstones which told of the departure in peace of so many Christians sleeping peacefully side by side—fathers, mothers,

sisters, and brothers ; and most touchingly a plot
she remembered, all by itself, of little children
(called God's acre), in which the forms of little
rosebuds had been broken off from the parent
stock to sleep till the resurrection morn.

She had a pious custom, on each Sunday morning, of shutting her eyes and reciting from memory
portions of the service, thus in imagination being
carried back to scenes of early childhood, and
joining in spirit with those who were still
worshiping in the old stone church, in chant
and song and praise.

She believed in the Apostles' Creed, and
" the communion of saints " was a token to her
that we are united with all Christians, living
or dead.

Estelle had thus been contemplating the rushing waters, that foamed as they rushed over large
rocks, and eddied round and round, with drift-
wood floating by—emblem of our lives often !—
not knowing where it would stop, whether by
the river's side, or on and on to the ocean, which,
like eternity, swallows up all that comes into its
bosom.

" Oh, if they only meet with success in their
enterprise, how glad I shall be ! and I can wait
in patience for their return."

Estelle's situation, out of sight of the cabin and her two protectors, was a dangerous one; at the same time, we must confess it was very romantic. The perils of the forest have often been depicted by our best American writers, and painted by our artists, some of whose sketches adorn the Capitol at Washington. One, with the title "Westward the Star of Empire takes its Way," shows bands of emigrants toiling over the mountains, with children in waggons and men on horseback; and there one sees how they took as much of the household stuff as they could carry. "The Noon Meal" shows how a large party have halted beside some cooling stream, and all surround the frugal meal in a circle, sitting on the grass; and one cannot help asking, what will be their fortune in a new home in the wilderness of the Far West? Then there is the "Baptism of Pocahontas," in a panel of the Rotunda, which represents the young Indian maiden who saved the life of Captain John Smith at the Indian slaughter near Jamestown, Virginia. Pocahontas, at the time Smith was lying on the ground to be executed, threw herself upon him, and begged his life at the hands of her father; and it was granted.

It was while Estelle was absent that a party, consisting of a middle-aged man and his wife and children, a boy and two girls, happened to be journeying from the Mohawk to the Owasco, and coming suddenly upon the cabin on the hill, were rejoiced to find a shelter for the night among their white brethren; and they were made heartily welcome.

As they were only sojourners for a night or so, we need not speak of them at great length; but, though not connected with the characters who have figured in our story, they do deserve mention, because the man became, many years after, the possessor of Fort Hill in connection with his farm, which lay close by it. This couple had, at an early day, left their paternal home in Massachusetts and Connecticut, and sought for a new one, in which they could rear their children and become possessors of the soil, which the Government allowed all citizens to take up and pay for in warrants issued to pay off the soldiers in the revolutionary war, in place of hard money, which in its poverty Government lacked. The Government issued a currency of paper bills, called continental money, and by some nicknamed " shin plasters."

Mr. Bostwick had early married a Connecticut lady named Hannah Warner; and being master of a trade—carpenter and cabinet-maker—he was able to construct a log house for himself, at a subsequent period, very near Fort Hill, and in which he opened a tavern to accommodate both "man and beast."

Although Estelle had not wandered far from the cabin, she was nearly exposed to a sudden surprise, and thus in danger. For, on looking across the stream, she saw a lot of Indians, who set up a yell which rang through the forest of evergreens, echoing far away over the hills. The Indians were evidently going to ford the stream. Quick as thought, she dropped behind the rock on which she was sitting, and began to crawl quietly towards some thick bushes of hemlock, and thence she ran as fast as she could to warn Allen and Bond of the approaching danger.

Both were greatly surprised at this sudden information; and they at once prepared to give the savages a warm reception. The rifles were loaded and primed; the flints carefully examined, and found to be all right. To make sure that nothing should be left undone, Estelle was directed to keep plenty of brush on the fire, and the big kettle of hot water ready to scald the head of the first Indian who put his head in the hole used for a window.

It was not long they had to wait in suspense after Estelle had arrived, for loud yells resounded again, and told of danger close at hand.

"Don't be afraid," said Allen; "we'll sell our lives dearly for you; and though they may outnumber us, we are a match for fifty of the redskins in our little castle."

Sinking down upon a chest, Estelle, the fair maiden, ejaculated a prayer to God to "defend them in all dangers and adversities," and "not to leave nor forsake them."

"Ah, yes," said Bond, "God will be your help now, for He has been your guide and rule of life since you were a little wee thing saying the Lord's Prayer at your mother's knee."

"The God of battles protect and defend us all, and deliver us out of the hands of our enemies!" cried she; and the other two said a hearty "Amen!"

A few moments sufficed to bring the rascals at the door, but it was strongly barricaded within.

"Do you hear them?" said Bond. "I suppose they mean business, though I can't understand their gibberish; and dang my buttons, but I'll give them some of my lead pills to cure their stomach-aches!"

Allen, who had followed the sea, took a quid of tobacco in his mouth—the better to steady his nerves, he said, a habit he had acquired on board of a man-of-war before going into action—and then he threw down his tarpaulin ready for the first onset.   He was a fine specimen of an American seaman, full-chested, with brawny arms, and quite six feet high in his stockings.

Bond seized his large sword, and stood behind Allen to finish his work, if needful. The window opening was only large enough for one to shoot out from at a time.

Poor Estelle, she spoke not a word, but her lips moved in silent prayer. She was greatly frightened, for she had heard how the Indians cruelly scalped their foes, and then killed them often by a slow torture. But she did not know that they had never been taught anything better, in their half-civilized condition, and their ignorant and depraved lives were pretty much on a footing with the wild beasts of the forest, with which they daily associated.

Bond felt assured that a good woman's prayers would be heard, and so he dismissed all fears of danger, though the yells became louder and fiercer than ever.

"Stand firm," said Bond to Allen; "they have

found us out, and yet they don't know but what we are twenty in number."

"Be sure of me, sir," replied the other. "I've stood more than one fight on the ocean, and I'll not flinch a hair now, with such a precious charge lying yonder."

The Indians, all at once, grew quiet, as if holding a council.

"It's no use trying to hold a parley with them, think you?" said Allen.

"Not much, I guess, from all I have heard about them, as they never ask or give quarter in fighting."

"Then, blast my eyes if I give them any mercy!"

"Mind, too, as men, we can't scalp them, as they will us, if they get a chance."

"Scalp us? what for?"

"Why, you see, none will ever get to be a big Indian chief, unless he has at least a dozen scalps dangling from his wampum belt."

On taking a peep through a hole just above the door, Allen saw the Indians drawing off stealthily, but looking back all the while, as if watching for some one to come out. At any rate, they evidently were bent on mischief.

This interval was filled up, in the mean time,

by the two men consulting what they would do if the Indians should set fire to their cabin and roast them out.

"Roast us out? How could they do that?" said Allen.

"Well, just as they roast a bear out of his cave. They build a fire in the mouth of the cave, and the smoke winds its way to Bruin's lair, and so he walks out to see what's the matter; and when he reaches the entrance, an Indian stands on one side, and strikes the bear on the head with his tomahawk. Then he soon despatches the cubs with a club, and eats them."

"And so that's what they call a fair fight?" said the sailor.

"Well, yes, I suppose so," said the other. "At all events, the bear doesn't know what killed him. Besides, the bear does not fight on very fair principles. He stands up, as if he would like to shake hands with a man and embrace him, and then he just hugs his victim to death!"

Not more than twenty minutes had elapsed before our imprisoned friends were startled by a loud outcry, rising into a wild scream, from the savages, which caused Estelle to tremble and beg, if it were possible, to treat with the Indians, "for," said she, "after all, they may not be bent on a hostile expedition."

"Don't you believe a word of it, miss," said Bruce. "They don't yell in that kind of style, unless they are seeking blood and plunder. No, no; they can talk as mild as a lamb when they come to beg coffee and tobacco, but that yell means a war-cry."

Then, all at once, as if by concert, the whole band set up a tremendous yell, which rang through the forest like a screech from a couple of locomotive engines. Determined to see the worst of the danger, Bond rushed out of the door, to see, only ten rods away, a band of fifty wild Indians, who, brandishing their tomahawks and knives in the air, and climbing over the earthworks, rushed towards the cabin.

They espied him at once, and he had just time to rush within the door and fix the barricade against it, when a dozen rushed madly forward, and planted their tomahawks into the door, with a yell that might have come from demons.

CHAPTER VI.

THE dangers which surrounded the two men
and poor Estelle were very threatening indeed.
Mr. Bostwick, his wife Hannah, and their three
children, were of little service, owing to their
inexperience of Indian habits and customs; and
although Mr. Bostwick was reared in Massachusetts, and his wife in Connecticut, where the
Indians had fought the Puritan settlers, they
knew nothing personally of Indian warfare.

Bond was the first to cheer up his companions,
now numbering in all eight; but the savage
yells soon drowned his words. Estelle had heard
enough to comfort her with the thought that
she was protected by three stout-hearted men,
and that the God of battles watched over them
all.

Bold as a lion, Bond was not content with
remaining pent up in the cabin. So, after being
wounded (as represented in the illustration), he
rushed forth, determined to overcome them by a
sudden display of courage. And, in truth, the

ATTACKED BY INDIANS.

[*Page* 128.

ammunition had nearly all been exhausted, so that he was obliged to seize his trusty sword, and deal death and destruction among the ranks of the wily foe. All aghast, the natives fell back with awful yells, as they saw the destruction of their chosen by one man. The slaughter on the right hand and on the left, by a dexterous movement of the white man, seemed to strike terror into the breasts of the savages, as he cut off one head after another and laid them low.

"Give them Jessie!" shouted Allen, as he laid about him on every side with a pike he had in his hand. "Remember our children and women in peril, and let us fight and die, if need be, in the last ditch!"

The Indians became demoralized by the terrible slaughter of their companions, and they began to think the Great Spirit had deserted them. They had their "charms" with them, but they began to fear that the pale-faces had charms also that protected them. For instance, they noticed that Bond wore a red cap with a feather in it. They imagined that if they could only capture this feather, the victory would turn on their side. They soon saw it was no use to fight against the "white man's medicine," * as it is called; and as

* A charm or talisman.

K

if by a signal, they began to withdraw, but in an orderly and quiet manner. They yelled and howled, making the forest ring out with their frightful noise. By striking their hands over their mouths, and yelling at the same time, they produced a horrid din, as any one can see who tries this mode, so common among all Indians, when having their war-dances.

For some time the forest echoed with their yells; but by-and-by they died away with the passing breeze, and all was hushed and still.

Mr. Bostwick, who had acted merely in the capacity of fugleman, or powder-man, doing good service, now exhorted the brave men to remember that, though they had shown great prowess in defending the helpless women and children, it was due to their heavenly Father to return thanks for so signal a deliverance.

All agreed to this pious proposition.

Drawing his Prayer-book from his pocket, he read from the psalter :—

"To Thee, O Lord our God, belong mercy and power, faithfulness and truth.

"Thou art our rock and our fortress, our deliverer, our God, our strength, in whom we will trust.

"We will call upon the Lord, who is worthy to

be praised; so shall we be saved from our enemies.

"We will keep the ways of the Lord our God for ever and ever, and He will be our guide unto death."

Then, drawing forth from another pocket a tuning-fork, and a pitch-pipe made of mahogany by himself, he began to sing, followed by his wife and others, the "Old Hundredth," so common all over the land.

> "Let all the earth, with one consent,
>   To God their cheerful voices raise ;
> Glad homage pay with awful mirth,
>   And sing before him songs of praise."

Then, kneeling down, they joined in the Lord's Prayer: and at the end of the prayer of thanksgiving, all said a hearty "Amen!"

While the inmates were preparing coffee for supper, which had been delayed to a late hour on account of the sudden attack of the Indians, Bond and Allen went out to take a survey of the battle-ground, and see how many of the savages had bitten the dust.

"The rascally villains!" muttered Bond, wiping the drops of perspiration from his brow, as he looked over the ground so recently covered with the dusky forms of the savages.

"Villains? I believe they are the children of the evil one," said the other, as he threw a quid of tobacco in the face of a dead Cayuga. "It's no child's play we've been engaged in, for every Indian is worse than a wild animal when he's a-fighting!"

"This fellow," said Bruce, pointing to a stalwart chief, "did not know what hit him, I guess, for a chunk of lead carried away the roof of his cranium."

"No, nor that other chap alongside him," said Allen, pointing to another whose body lay apart from his head. "You must have read of Sir William Wallace, the hero of Scotland, who swung his claymore, fifteen feet long, and cut his way in many a fray among the Highlands, as a mower cuts the grain."

"And you? Why give me all the praise? You thrashed the rascals as though you had swung a flail all your life on a farm."

"Ay, ay," said the sailor, "I played a tattoo on some of their skulls, and gave them what Paddy gave the drum—a good beating."

Supposing the other Indians might return in the night to bury the bodies of the slain, or carry them off, they took advantage of the moonlight to count them, and found a dozen lying prostrate on the ground. They had gone to "the happy hunting grounds " for good and all.

But the drama was not yet ended. Bond saw one of the biggest of the Indians raise himself up gradually from the ground, and he drew near to see if he needed another touch of the weapon he had left in the cabin ; but when he came close to the Indian, he jumped up suddenly, and with a yell plunged his knife into Bond's side, and so, before he could say " Jack Robinson," bounded away and was out of sight. Judge of Bond's surprise, which was so sudden as almost to paralyze him ; and turning to his friend, he said—

" Dang my buttons ! but the fellow came near giving me my quietus. If he had aimed a little higher, he'd have struck a deadly blow."

" Are you seriously hurt ? " said Allen.

" Not exactly—only my ' bread-basket ' is cut a little near the diaphragm ; and I hope to live yet to give him a Roland for an Oliver."

" Lucky he didn't stay longer and strike higher. He could easily have finished you ; but I'd have taken the wind out of his sails," said the other.

" If he had fired the magazine "—pointing to his heart—" he'd have blown me up sky high."

They now began to look more carefully at the others, lest another one or two might be still alive and "playing 'possum." But they were satisfied that nothing could revive the carcases of those remaining stark and stiff upon the ground, till the trumpet of the archangel should sound at the resurrection morn.

On their return to the cabin, they found that in the excitement Mr. Bostwick had been slightly wounded, and that Estelle had bound his wrist with a bandage during the fight. As he had not complained at all, Bond and Allen had not known it before. After this excitement, Estelle had thrown herself down upon her rude bed, and seemed to fall into a kind of stupor. When they entered the cabin, she revived, and exclaimed in an excited manner—

"Heavenly Father! are we safe?"

"Safe as a bug in a rug," said Bond. "We've laid a dozen low, and many more must have gotten away wounded."

"And are you quite sure they are really gone off for good?"

"Yes; all that could travel have gone to tell their sorrowful tale. But if they had set eyes on you, they might have fought more desperately, to have added you to the chief's household, and made you Queen of the Cayugas."

"Heaven forbid!" exclaimed she, with a shudder.

To convince her that all was peaceful without, he led her forth to look upon the scene of slaughter.

A BIT OF ROMANCE.

She soon came upon one of the fallen foe. The moonlight enabled her to look upon the face of one upturned to the sky, and what most attracted her notice was a cap made of the feathers of a white swan, such as she had seen upon the heads of the most noted chiefs, as distinguished from those made from squirrel-skins and foxes. The expression on the face of the Indian at once aroused her attention, as if by magic. There is something startling and awful in looking upon the face of the dead at any time; but there is a difference in the appearance of one who dies after a spell of sickness and long suffering, and one who is suddenly cut off in full health. Hence in paintings depicting the scene of "Herodias's daughter bearing the head of John the Baptist in a charger," one will notice a waxlike appearance of the skin.

The Indian lay half doubled up, with one arm under his head and the right hand of the other thrust into his bosom, as if grasping something half concealed.   Perhaps it was only a woman's curiosity that noticed this circumstance.   She looked at him, almost fearing to draw his hand away ; for he was lying close by eleven others, and any one looking upon these slaughtered men would say to themselves, as she did, " These savages have done nothing that seemed wrong for them to do.   They kill all foes, wild beasts and birds, white and red men, because they learn in infancy that a good Indian must be a brave, or he will never get to be a chief.   They," said she, " were alive an hour ago, and now they have gone to the other world, to be judged by their Creator according to the light of nature as their only teacher.   God made them as well as He made us, and He is a merciful Father to all His children."

The dead Indian who awakened these reflections had his face partly covered by long black, silken hair, falling below his neck to the shoulders.

As her feelings of horror gradually subsided from the first sight of the slain natives lying around him, she stooped over the body, and gently took hold of the hand that seemed clenched with a death grip on a part of his body.   The fingers were not stiff, but yielded easily to her effort to unclasp them from the spot they were fastened, and the hand fell instantly to the ground. The sudden unclosing of the fingers made her start, and she thought she perceived a kind of quivering of the body to take place. Pausing a moment, she watched the body, but could perceive nothing further that indicated life. At length, putting her hand upon the spot on his bosom, she felt something beneath his vesture of a hard substance. Curiosity at once induced her to take a small clasp knife which she had for years carried with her, and to cut through the cloth. In doing this she discovered a small silver plate, fastened with strings of some kind of skin, which went through holes in it, and then passed round his body and were tied strong.

With considerable difficulty she unfastened the plate, and drew it from beneath the covering. The outside was polished bright and smooth, and the under side was hollow ; the plate being raised in similar form to the crystal of a watch, but filled with something resembling rosin or pitch.

The cause of this being worn upon his body she could not divine. In vain she examined the spot from whence she had removed it, to discover if it had shielded a tender point or scar ; but there was nothing on the skin but the impress which it had seemingly made by being compressed with the tightness of the leather cords that had fastened it. If it was for ornament, why should the wearer have concealed it beneath the cloth vestment ? And it could have been no protection as a shield to his body, it was so small; and, in addition, it covered no particularly exposed point of his body which might lead one to suppose it placed there for a breastplate.

Musing a few moments on the singularity of the circumstance, she put the plate into her bosom, and rose to leave the body. As she was about turning to depart, she thought she would again ascertain, for a certainty, if there was life in him; and, accordingly, once more bent herself over the inanimate form before her. Thrusting her hand into his bosom, she placed her soft palm upon his heart. Scarce had she touched this spot, the seat of life, when a faint exclamation escaped her ; for beneath her gentle pressure, she distinctly felt a feeble throbbing, as though life, still lingering, was about passing off in fainter and fainter pulsations from the vital throne. " The dying spark still glows," murmured she to herself, withdrawing her hand from his bosom, and, raising his head, attempted to place him in an easier position.

As she moved him, the hand that she first discovered grasping his breast was convulsively raised by him to the same spot from which she had unloosed it, and seemed vainly attempting to clasp the place again. In raising his head, a part of his dishevelled long hair fell back and exposed his face, and for the moment he opened his eyes. There was a languid mildness in their expression as they fixed upon her bending over him, and his lips moved as if attempting to articulate something, although no sound caught her ear. That feeling, inherent in the female bosom, which neither time nor circumstances can eradicate, and which ever shows itself at the sight of distress, prompted Estelle to alleviate the suffering form before her. To save life, though at the hazard of bringing a deadly foe again upon them, altered not her sympathetic heart ; and she chafed the cold forehead of the native, and applied a small vial of camphorated and volatile spirits, carried and used by herself, to his nostrils, to revive, if possible, the almost inanimate form she was bending over. Again he opened his eyes, a new life seemed to have been given to the dark orbs of vision, and a faint smile apparently played upon his countenance ; consciousness was first usurping the suspended powers of animation.

Mentally Estelle thanked the omnipotent God,

as she saw indications of returning life, brought as it were into existence again, by the slender means she was enabled to use. A small tree stood near where he lay stretched upon the ground; and she exerted her utmost strength to move and set him leaning against it. She succeeded, and for a moment sat by his side, holding his head, which had dropped from feebleness upon one side; and while supporting him in this upright position, Bond and Allen came upon the scene.

To those who have witnessed woman's devotion at the bedside of the sick and dying, of the sick and wounded in hospitals, and on the battle-field of deadly strife, Estelle's attention to this one is easily understood. Florence Nightingale, at the Crimean war, was the forerunner of many others rising up in the civil war in America, as also in the Prussian and French campaign, ready to go forth and smooth the pathway of the dying to the better land. Indeed, many a youth was restored to loved mother by careful nursing of those Sisters of Mercy, or better called, "Merciful Sisters," in some army hospital.

Bond asked Estelle if she expected to restore again to life one he deemed "as dead as a stone."

"My friend, do you not see that life is not ex-

tinct? This young savage still breathes, and God
will be angry with us if we do not try to preserve his life now he is in our power."

" No doubt, madam; but if he *be* alive, he
reminds me of a cat, which, they say, has nine
lives."

" I certainly thought him dead at first," said
she, " but on moving him he began to show signs
of life. Run to the cabin, and fetch me the wine
cordial, do; I think he can be saved."

" But," said the other, " mercy is not justice.
' Let the dead bury the dead,' says the Bible."

" Scripture says also, ' Thou shalt not kill,' and
' Mercy rejoiceth against judgment.' "

Bond soon got the cordial.

"Pray," said Allen, "let's save the wounded and
bury the dead. I've been a prisoner myself and
was wounded, so I know how it is. If the
English surgeon hadn't been kind to me on a
man-of-war ship, where would I be now? It
was me that felled the chap, and the young
Indian smiled as he drew near, when I was cutting right and left. He fell, as if a ball had
reached his heart, and he only gave a faint yell,
and all at once was as still as a dead kitten."

Estelle applied the cordial to his lips, and at
once they removed him a short distance, and laid

him carefully down upon a bed of dry leaves. Next, they laid the bodies of his eleven companions in a trench, throwing evergreens over them, and then covering them with the light sandy soil of the hill.

Night was setting in, and, as yet, Walker and the captain had not returned. The sun went down in the west, reflecting a gorgeous sunlight on the tree-tops and over the distant hills which towered up in the north.

The spot where the bodies of the slain lay they marked with stakes, and the men at once gathered some dry branches with which to make a fire, and keep it burning through the night, in case the captain should return hungry, and might need, at least, a cup of coffee, if not a rasher of bacon or a piece of dried venison.

" I shouldn't wonder," said Bond, " that some ugly customer will pay us a visit to-night. The smell of blood is very keen among beasts of the forest; and it is said that crows and buzzards can scent a carcase five miles away."

" Well," said Allen, " we must stow away our dried venison and moose-meat " (meaning the supposed dead Indian who had been nursed by Estelle).

But she came back from the bed of leaves upon

which the young Indian lay, and reported that he had suddenly revived and made his escape, without as much as thanking her for her kindness, or telling her when he would come back again. She said he darted into the forest like a deer, and bounded away as if nothing was the matter.

This led to a consultation as to what was best to be done.

" If," said one of them, " the fellow is not a viper you've warmed into life, he'll be glad he has gotten off with a whole skin. On the contrary, if he has any gratitude in him, we have nothing to fear. Doubtless, he can soon reach the Cayuga Lake, and bring back upon us a host of savages, but all we have to do is to keep a good look-out, and not be caught napping."

Estelle retired to her couch, musing on the strange events of the day, and tried to compose herself for a good night's rest.

In the mean time her companions were in any mood but that of sleeping, and they resolved that their eyes should not for a moment be closed that night. They mutually kept each other wide awake by talking, now of the day's adventure, and next of scenes far away at the east they called their home.

"Catch me," said Allen, "venturing my life with our captain in a dense forest again, with wild cats and wild Indians. It is too much like Alexander Selkirk and his island, we used to sing of—

> ' I am monarch of all I survey,
>   My right there is none to dispute;
>   From the centre all round to the sea,
>   I am lord of the fowl and the brute.'

No, no; give me the smell of salt water, and plenty of clams and oysters (quahogs some call them), lobsters and shad, in preference to all the dried venison, and the glory of dead Indians thrown into the bargain."

"I was in hope," replied the other, "that the captain and the others would put in an appearance and solve the mystery ere this; and even now, it seems to me, I hear some steps coming this way."

"Maybe it's them," replied Allen.

But how mistaken! All at once they found themselves surrounded and held down by a fresh lot of savages, who began at once to bind their limbs with some green withes they had brought with them. Here, indeed, was a sudden surprise!

"Well," grumbled the old sailor, "dang my buttons, this is quick work, friend Bond," whom he saw prostrate, and in the same predicament with himself.

The stealthy, snake-like approach of the Indians, surprising the two bold men (Mr. Bostwick and wife having made their escape through the aid of a friendly Indian), did not prevent their calm consideration of the situation. They might, indeed, feel soon the tomahawk or scalping knife in their heads with deadly effect; but, somehow or other, they did not easily give way to depression or despair. They felt more interested in poor Estelle, as one of the savages was seen to catch hold of her the moment she had reached the spot where her protectors lay, helpless to defend her.

Her captor bound her hands behind her and led her into the cabin. The Indians appeared in no hurry, but were cool and collected.

A tall, fine-looking young Indian led the band of twelve young warriors, and his orders were strictly obeyed. As near as the prisoners could catch the words, he said —

" EAU-HIYA-KSUWEYA-CUICA-WIKOSKA ; KIN-CUICA-TARINEA ! "

That is, "Do not hurt the young maiden, the young deer."

L

One of the Indians asked what they should do with the " IMKTOMI-HUHA-KANSKAS-KA ; " that is "*Daddy long-legs*," as they called the two men.

But they set up such a jabbering in the language of the Iroquoi, that it was hard to tell what it all meant, as neither had picked up any bits of the Indian language. But so, too, they knew very well the Indians did not, on their part, understand the English language ; so they freely exchanged views on their perilous condition.

" Confound their lingo ! " said Allen. " Why don't they speak like Christians, and not let their words jerk out through their teeth and noses ? My opinion is it's worse than dog Latin ; and I shouldn't wonder if they don't understand it themselves ! "

" You'd better dry up, old fellow," replied the other. " Don't you see the rascals are building a fire yonder, as if they meant to stay and make themselves at home here, and maybe roast us alive, as an offering to the 'Great Manitou' ? "

" Well," said Allen, " they know one word at least besides 'whisky' (*miniwakan*), and that is 'Yankee,' pronounced by them ' *Yengeese*,' and the way they learned to call us so is thus explained. The French in Canada had much to say to the Indians about their foes, the English, and that was as near as they could pronounce the word."

They both began to feel pain in their arms and legs, as the green withes which bound them were very tightly tied.

"Can't you get one of your flippers loose, and cut my lashings ? "

"Devil a bit of it ! " replied the old sailor. " My opinion is, if you call on them to loosen your stays, they'll cut your throat from ear to ear."

Thus they talked on to each other to while away the time, and evidently to cheer themselves up—as naughty boys, who are put in a dark room for punishment, are said to whistle to keep up their courage. And all the while they kept a sharp look upon the Indians, watching every motion as they were making preparations to pass the night outside the cabin. So they felt re-assured that their lives would be spared, at least for a while, when they saw the savages throw themselves on the ground where they had spread their skins, and were soon snoring loudly. The moon shone out through the clouds, and the heat-lightnings played across the western sky, but did not disturb their slumbers.

CHAPTER VII.

New revelations and some startling scenes now lie before us, in our story of the early day on Fort Hill.

Bond and Allen could not sleep long nor very sound, and, after being left to themselves, wondered why the Indians should have become, as it were, unmindful of them. It had thundered and the lightning had flashed, but no rain had fallen to wet their skins. Then they began to make efforts to loosen their bonds, which bound them so tightly. If they could only loosen them, they could contrive some plan of escape while the thunder howled, and the mire would not reveal their walking to Estelle's cabin to try and release her. But they failed, as the withes were green and tied too tight to let them get a leg or arm loose to use them.

"Well," said the old sailor, "I suppose we may as well make the best of it. Let us try and got a little more sleep on the dry leaves, and do as 'The Babes in the Wood' did when they had no home to live in."

But the other partner in danger had no heart to indulge in witticism or jokes while surrounded with dangerous foes, who might take it into their heads to get up at any moment, and sacrifice them by roasting slowly before a fire, or torture them by fastening them to a tree and practising their skill in throwing knives or tomahawks at their heads, by way of shooting at a mark.

But nature will give way to fatigue, and it was not long before both were fast asleep once more, and snoring too, as soundly as if they were at home sleeping in a stable, or on board ship swinging in a hammock.

Allen next morning, on opening his eyes, discovered a large stalwart Indian standing directly over him, and gazing intently at him. He seemed to look down upon his captives with silent contempt, much as a huge mastiff contemplates a little terrier, or as a cat looking at a mouse. His broad, naked shoulders, and arms muscular and sinewy, folded upon his bosom, showed a strength not to be despised, and his gaze denoted a vision like the eagle's as he gazes upon the sun.

Allen raised himself on his elbow, and turned

up his good-natured but rather doleful face to the captor, and said, "Old chap, just you cut these things and let me loose, and I'll not run away, 'pon my honour."

No answer to Allen's request was returned by the native, who seemed not to understand him ; but strode off with a majestic tread, after having gathered up a large bearskin partly over his shoulders, which had fallen low about his body as he stood with his folded arms over the old sailor.

"Stiff as a midshipman!" muttered Allen. "If I had you on board the *Butterfly*, my copper-coloured chap, the boatswain should tickle your hull;" and he followed him with his eyes as he mingled with the other natives, who were now stirring round.

It was an hour or two after this before any of the natives took notice of Bond or Allen. They had both risen to a sitting posture, and hitched themselves close together. Bond would occasionally utter a curse against the imps, which would immediately be responded to by the other. All at once, they discovered a cluster of natives gathering together, and in a few moments they came towards where they sat. As they moved along, a white man was seen among them, though he looked about as savage as the crowd of dark bodies around him.

"There is a white Indian among them fellows," said Bond.

"So there is, or old Bob never took a correct observation," replied Allen. "I wonder if the fellow has turned Turk or Indian?"

"Very likely both," answered Bond.

In the mean time the crowd of natives approached where they were sitting, and soon surrounded them by forming a circle. As yet they had kept strict silence, but all of a sudden a yell proceeded from the leader, and all joined in the horrid chorus. Then they began to move round in single file, uttering sounds of discord; while each one lifted his tomahawk, and drew his scalping knife, flourishing them in the air, and with fiendish looks directed towards their prisoners, strained their voices as loud as thunder.

Old Allen eyed them as they danced around, like the witches in "Macbeth," until his face relaxed into a quizzical smile at the comic actions and queer doings he saw. But turning to Bond, he muttered, "Dang my buttons, Master Bond, what under the sun are they about?"

"Well," replied he, "I guess it means our death song, and they are chanting it now."

"I do not fancy the music," replied Allen; "and it can't be true, as some old poet wrote—

' Music hath charms to soothe the savage breast;'

for they are singing our lullaby, and stirring up the old boy in their wicked hearts." The eyes of Allen rolled from one object to another, while they circled round with their faces horribly painted. "Confound their tin-pan music! It sounds about as musical as filing a saw, or pulling a naughty cat out of an ash-hole! Now, if they put daylight through me, and *you* get off, you tell our captain that I died game."

The loud yells of the savages almost drowned this appeal; but Bond had nodded assent, as his bold comrade made a successful attempt to get his hand loose. Having a large pocket-knife in his left side pocket, he managed to work it out, and with his teeth opened the blade. One may be sure he was not long in cutting himself loose. He was free from the withes which held him fast. Turning to his comrade, he whispered, "I may as well let you up too, and see if we can't get out of this hell-hole!"

Then he cut the other's fastenings, undiscovered by the Indians—at least, they thought so. But the two men were imprudent enough to draw out a plug of tobacco, and while Allen was biting off a quid, the Indians discovered the motion. All of a sudden, a dozen sprang up, and raising their tomahawks, began to yell and whoop like mad. They would soon have made short work of their prisoners, had not the tall and muscular savage, and another (a youth), with a bound jumped in before them, ordering them back to where they had just been seated.

The chief ordered the prisoners to follow him ; and they rose to their feet, wondering what next would take place. Harmless they went with him on the other side of the hollow, a few rods, where Estelle was a prisoner, and were bid to enter.

"Ah, Bond, we had a close shave that time," said Allen. "We'd have soon been done for —made cold mutton, I'm sure, if they did not really torture us over a slow fire."

"Yes, that's so," replied Bond. "But where is Estelle ? I pray Heaven she's not carried off beyond our reach."

Before Allen had time to reply, the poor girl, pale and agitated, entered the shelter and sank down, with her hands tied fast behind her. She had passed the night quite unharmed, indeed, but sleep refused to visit her eyelids. The loud shouts of the savages had driven her from the tent a few minutes before, but seeing her friends safe, she came back again.

"Bless your dear heart, miss," said the old sailor, "I was afraid we would never see your face again."

"Thanks be to Him who hath said, 'not a hair of your head shall perish,' we are all thus far safe from cruel torture and death. But," said she, "those natives who were slain yesterday will be visited upon us, I greatly fear."

"Never you mind, girl," said Allen. "Things look squally; but, you know, we must have a gale now and then, for the sea is purified by winds and storms, and it is not always calm and smooth, nor is it ever fair weather at all times on the ocean. But, dear me, let me cut your arms loose."

"No, no," said she. "I am afraid they will bind me tighter still if you do."

If any one has heard a loud crash of thunder and seen forked lightning break out of a black sky, he can imagine how startled this group was when they heard another outcry from the Indians, which excelled all they had heard before. It brought the men to their feet, and not knowing the cause, they rushed at once to the opening of the tent to see what had caused this tumult.

The natives were all rushing along the south part of the trenches, with fiendish shouts, jumping over the parapets close by the prisoners. All at once they heard the loud bark of Bose, the captain's dog, a huge mastiff well known to the old sailor.

"Ah," said he, "our comrades have returned, I feel quite sure." I hear old Bose's loud bark;" and he started at once for the tent door to see if it was really true.

The tall Indian pushed him back, and placed himself in front of the door of the tent.

The old salt gave a horrified look as he was thus pushed back, and he hardly knew what next to do, so he wisely resigned himself to his fate.

Presently, however, Bose came bounding in, jumping up to kiss the faces of all his friends.

"Where can the captain be?" said Estelle.

As soon as the old sailor could quiet the faithful dog, he said to her, "Yes, he can't be far away;" and the girl trembled as she sat and listened to the yells of the Indians, for she knew not if a deadly combat had already begun.

"The natives have captured our friends, I am quite sure," said Allen.

"Yes, indeed," replied the other; "and so we must all die without judge or jury."

Amid the loud yells and awful screams that rang through the forest, the old sailor and his friend chafed in spirit that they could not have a share or hand in the fray, when suddenly the tent was parted and the captain, with Walker and Sambo, the black servant, tightly bound, and their clothes besmeared with blood, were thrust in.

"More prisoners!" said the captain, as his hand was grasped by the old sailor.

"Ay, ay, sir, it is true. But they had double the number of us; and though old Allen has been a prisoner before, these fellows can't make me scare worth a cent. Ha! old sable," continued he, turning to his black companion in misery, who was covered with blood and looking pale round the mouth, "I'm glad to see you haven't lost your scalp."

This sally of wit cheered up Sambo, and he grinned from ear to ear as he said, "Dis nigger wasn't brought up in de woods to be scared by owls." But the old darkey would have been glad to see the whole crew of savages drowned in the Owasco Lake.

From the opening of the tent in front, they could see something of what was going forward among the aborigines, as a large lot of them had gathered together, and one of them could be heard haranguing the rest. Next, the crowd separated, and very soon they beheld the bodies of those slain by Bond and Allen taken up and carried away. As the last one passed in single file, Bond told the captain all about the battle they had been engaged in, and of the flight of the natives, and how they were taken prisoners by surprise and bound as captives.

In the mean time, Walker was rehearsing to Estelle something which caused her to weep. For a short time after this, Walker and the captain whispered together apart, and it was seen that the stern features of the captain relaxed, and a smile came over his manly, sunburnt features.

The day passed off in a quiet monotony, and quite a number of dusky faces passed every now and then, viewing the tent; and it was observed that a powerful, tall, and muscular-built native kept quite close to them, and he glanced often at each of the prisoners.

At the same time a number of others were engaged in erecting lodges of bark, as though they intended sojourning there for some time longer. The old man Allen and the black now began to think they were in no immediate danger, and at once set to tell old yarns they had learned at sea, sometimes fighting pirates arm to arm in the Spanish main, or singing the song of

"Captain Kidd, Captain Kidd,
How he sail-ed, how he sail-ed,"

etc., etc.   They, as thousands of others, believed the pirate's story of having buried untold treasures of silver somewhere on the shores of Long Island, near "Coney Island," or at Rockaway.

The sunrise next morning found all in the tent wide awake, and the natives bustling about making preparations for some coming event, quite mysterious.   A number were carefully examining their bows and arrows, while some were listening to one of the chiefs, who was gesticulating and speaking in a low voice.

The captain watched him, as did Walker also, with some forebodings of coming evil.   Walker knew full well the spirit of all Indians, who hold the old Mosaic teaching of an " eye for an eye, and a tooth for a tooth," *i.e.*, blood for blood ; and some, if not all the party there, must suffer the penalty of death.

Strange, that of all, Sambo showed the least anxiety or emotion.   He would scan the features and forms of the redskins as they passed to and fro where they were, while now and then he would curse them as worse than pirates on the ocean.

They had not long to wait before they were informed as to their fate.

" It is all up with us," said one of them.

When death threatens, or any severe danger is at hand, we first begin to think of dear loved ones at home, who will suffer all the horrors attending upon our decease, while waiting hour after hour, day by day, and month after month, in hopeless anxiety as to our fate, wondering if we will ever return again to gladden the fireside of old home!

The sun was high up in the sky, when all of a sudden the Indians began to surround the tent. They brought out each of its inmates one by one, and fastened them by withes singly to large beech trees, and then a kind of war-dance began. The trees were all in a row, so each had a view of his companions.

The yelling increased in louder tones, as though the Indians were working themselves up to a higher pitch of excitement and rage. Then they began shooting their arrows into the trees just above the heads of their victims, and now and then a tomahawk would be hurled in the same direction, sticking fast in the bark of the tree.

Poor Estelle was taken to the tree next the captain, and her arms were fastened around the trunk, while she seemed ready to faint with fear. Bond and the black man were tied to two trees next, and Allen, Walker, and Bostwick came next in order. Here they stood in breathless anxiety for a whole hour, awaiting death. Visions of horror and torture were passing through their minds all the while, ere death should come to release them from their cruel foes. But a surprise on which they had not counted now awaited them.

Just as they had given up all hope of relief and could endure no longer the horrid suspense, and while all (save Estelle, who was less moved than any) trembled with anxiety, a tall, powerful native—the one who had thrust the captain into the tent so hastily—accompanied by a light, straight, youthful, fine-built native, with two white men dressed in full Indian costume, presented themselves before the eyes of the astonished prisoners. They had suddenly leaped over the parapet right in front of the captives, and hurried towards them. Here was a surprise indeed ! The whole scene changed as if wrought by a miracle.

Upon this the savages broke forth anew in a

yell of fierce anger, as they witnessed this interruption of what they would call sport. A fierce conflict was impending, as the Indians raised their weapons in defiance; but the chief placed a bugle to his lips, and blowing a blast, ordered silence. A moment more, and he rushed to the side of the nearest prisoner and cut his bonds loose, and so on to the others.

Had an angel suddenly come down from heaven to release them, he could not have been more of a surprise and a welcome deliverer. They stared at the chief, but had no words to express their amazement.

In a moment, however, Walker sprang forward, and addressed one of the whites who came, saying, "Thank Heaven, she" (Estelle) "is saved ! Behold your daughter !"

These words, like a new revelation, struck upon the ears of Estelle, as she rushed forward and threw herself into the arms of her newly found and long-lost father. She exclaimed, " Oh, my dear, dear father, I thought you were dead and I an orphan !"

He could only sob out, " My child, my only daughter !" and as the tears rolled down his bronzed cheeks, he drew her near his bosom and thanked God, with uplifted hand to heaven, for

M

that sacred hour.   It seemed to him like a dream, as he gazed from the captain to Walker, and for a moment seemed lost in thought.

After Estelle's emotion had had full vent, and her usual calm repose had returned, she released her hold of her parent, and glanced at the youthful native who had cut their bonds and set them free.   His eye was riveted on her, as he advanced with hand extended, and at once threw himself at her feet in adoration, thanking her, in English, as his preserver—the one who had saved his life.

Estelle recognized him as the youthful native whom she had begged Bond and Allen to spare during the recent battle, and then, with her own hands, had restored him to life among the mutilated remains of those of his comrades whose lifeless forms strewed the ground on Fort Hill.

Putting her hand into her bosom, she drew forth the silver medal which she had taken from his body when he was unconscious, and handed it to him.   He took it with eagerness, kissing and grasping it as his greatest earthly treasure.

Allen drew near him, having seen Estelle hand the medal to the young man.

" Let me look at that for a moment, my boy,"

said he, at the same time wiping his eyes with his sleeve.

Just then, the white man who came with Estelle's father rushed forward, his eyes nearly bursting out of his head, and stood by their side. On seeing what was in the hand of Allen, he made a faint attempt to clasp the young Indian in his arms; and with a half exclamation in these words, " Oh, my dear, dear——." fell back insensible to the ground.

And thus ended, for the day, the romance of Fort Hill.

CHAPTER VIII.

WE left our heroine, the beautiful Estelle, and party surprised in Fort Hill by the sudden release of herself and the other prisoners bound to trees and expecting sudden death. During the time that this occurred, the black man, Sam, had remained speechless, staring at the tall young Indian. Suddenly he threw up his arms, and exclaimed—

" I declare to goodness, Bob Allen, that's

massa! I knows him by the colour of de eyes! Sure's you live, now, it's young Massa Charlie, for de scars on his cheek is dar, sure as gospel, mind I tell ye."

Bob replied, " Well, old Snowball, I guess you're right;" and then he proceeded to hug the stranger tight as a bear, exclaiming, "Can't you see I'm your old mate Bob?"

The gallant youth stood for a moment as if hesitating in doubt, bewildered by what he had seen ; but soon recovering his self-possession, said, " Yes, I do remember. But who is this?" pointing to the man prostrate before him.

" Blast my eyes if I know!" said the old sailor. " Perhaps it's some chap turned Indian, the same as you and Estelle's father."

Then the captain and the darkey stood a little way off, the black holding something in his hand which he was trying to decipher. "Show it to him, captain"—pointing to the supposed Master Charlie. "It seems to me dey bof look just alike."

Before the captain could reply, Estelle's father approached and demanded, " Where did you find that ?"

" Up in the eagle's nest, massa. He climb the tree, and grab it in his hand," replied the black.

" Hush up, you rascal, you black ace of spades !"

said Allen, as he approached the captain. " Do you see that copper-coloured na-*tive?*" pointing to the young savage.

" I do; but what about him?" said the captain.

" Well, nothing; *only he happens to be your* own brother—turned Indian for the time being, that's all."

" My eyes!" exclaimed the captain. " Has he the counterpart of this? " seizing the medallion from the darkey, and placing it by the side of the one he held.

" Stand back!" said Estelle's father. " I alone can explain all of this."

Now, to help to understand this part of our story, I will explain to my youthful readers the following, as relating to the early part of the narrative.

The Continental Congress, which met first in Philadelphia, and adopted the title of

"THE UNITED STATES OF AMERICA,"

had a very few vessels of war to constitute her navy. Among those who figured among the boldest and bravest of men was Paul Jones.

This man, who became conspicuous in our

struggles for independence, was a Scotchman, born at Arbigland, near the mouth of the river Nith, 6th of July, 1747. In 1779 Jones was placed in command of an expedition, under the joint auspices of the King of France and the American Commissioners.

A short account of this brave man will be found in the Appendix, as well as a sketch of the life of Davy Crockett, a warrior on land.

Jones had a naval battle with several of the king's men of war, and a small continental cruiser managed to sail away into New England, and this vessel fell in with a wreck, which was boarded by one of her boats.

When the leader first jumped upon the deck, not a living person was seen. But on entering the cabin, however, a handsome lady was found almost dead of starvation, and lying beside her were two male children, aged only a few months. There was just enough of life in her emaciated form for her to speak to her discoverers, telling them who she was, and the names of the dear little ones she was so soon to leave to the care of strangers. Breathing a prayer for them, she then expired.

There was little of value found on the vessel, and after sewing up the delicate body of the poor lady, they consigned her remains to the great deep, with this prayer :—

" We therefore commit her body to the deep, to be turned into corruption, looking for the resurrection of the body (when the sea shall give up her dead), and the life of the world to come, through our Lord Jesus Christ : who at His coming shall change our vile body, that it may be like His glorious body, according to the mighty working whereby He is able to subdue all things unto Himself."

One said, " Did you ever think what a singular expression that is, taken from Scripture—'The sea shall give up the dead ' ? "

The children were taken on board the yacht, and two men selected to care for them : one of them was the black, Sambo, and the other the large-hearted Yankee Allen. These children had had no sustenance for several days, save what they drew from an open vein in the mother's arm—they sapping her own life-blood to sustain themselves, and fulfilling Bible language, " Can the mother forget her sucking child ? "

Black Sam first discovered this; and it was said that the sailors amused themselves some-times, while the cruiser was making port, by pricking their fingers and letting the little fellows suck the blood.

The mother had fastened two silver medals round her children's necks, the name of each loved one being engraved thereon; and in order to preserve the medals, the sailor and the black had encased them in leather pouches covered with wax, which they tied to the orphans' bodies.

In a few days they were in sight of land, and the little fellows were taken ashore, and duly cared for.

After a year or so, one of them strayed away, or perhaps was stolen, and no trace of him could be found.

The other one, after two or more years, was taken on board the cruiser as an accepted child of the ocean (they called him " the little man-of-war's-man "), with a view to educate him for the navy. The name graven on his medal, which he lost just before his brother was missing, was "Willie Williamson ; " and on his being placed on board the cruiser, Allen, in order to preserve his name in case of any accident, did what so many sailors do — tattooed the letters on the boy's breast with Indian ink, pricked in with a needle.

Now let us return to the day when the other twin boy was missing, and explain who were the other persons spoken of at Fort Hill.

Estelle was the daughter of Edmund Griffith, who, several years before our story begins, had left civilization and plunged into the forests of the Far West, in search of adventure and of fortune. He was living in what was called "a howling wilderness," but which to-day is dotted with those beautiful towns and cities along the Mohawk, the Genesee, and the Susquehanna.

Estelle's mother had died when she was an infant and knew little or nothing of a proud mother's love and tenderness, and so her maternal aunt had the little one adopted into her own family.

The father of Estelle, as soon as her mother was dead, left the banks of the Yantic river, in Connecticut, and for a long time no one knew what had become of him. Then, about that time, the twin brother of Willie was seen to be missing, and after a vain attempt to ascertain his whereabouts, it was concluded that the poor little one must have strayed to the river's bank and got drowned.

As time, however, rolled along, Estelle had reached her sixteenth year, and Walker, the only son of those who adopted her, had already arrived at the age of manhood. He had joined some fur traders under the advice of Mr. Astor, who was the prime mover and most influential

of the "North American Fur Company." He
started westward in hopes of winning fame and
fortune, hunting with the French Canadians and
the Indians along the St. Lawrence and other
rivers, up south to the tributaries of the Owasco
and Cayuga lakes.

He suddenly made his appearance one day in
his eastern home, whither his steps had eagerly
turned, to give the glad tidings that Estelle's
father had been found and was then living in
the west. It was in a vast forest of beeches
on the western shores of the Owasco that he
had providentially come across her father, who
was leading somewhat of a hermit's life, in a log
cabin lined with wolf and bear skins.

Walker had learned from Estelle's father that
the missing orphan had been carried off by him,
and had remained with him as a constant companion for a long time, until at last he had been
stolen from him in an unguarded moment, while
he was absent, or perhaps had been devoured by
some wild beast of the forest, so many of which
had a habit of prowling about ready to devour
man or beast, if once secure of their prey. He
searched the woods for a long time, but no trace
of him could be found. When this happened,
he naturally was afraid to return to his native

place, and so he remained buried alive, as it were, in the almost desert wilds of the Owasco country.

At the time of Walker's return, Williamson, the sailor, who had risen to be a captain in the Continental Navy service, had arrived again in port and heard the marvellous story of Walker. A new feeling wno took possession of his breast; one desire only animated him, and that was, to seek out his long-lost brother. He would see, also, if he could bring back Estelle's father to his old haunts of civilization.

At once preparations were made by Captain Williamson for absence on his cruiser, the *Butterfly*, which had conveyed them by the Long Island Sound, through Hurl Gate (a dangerous place, full of whirlpools and rocks), on to Manhatten Island, off New Amsterdam (now New York), where he took passage to visit the new settlements on the shores of Lake Ontario.

Here the real development of my story begins to unfold itself. Captain Williamson had arrived at the fort, and formed one of the group which were gazing at the medal.

"Ah, yes!" said he, "I am sure it must be my dear brother, for though I have not seen him since we were little shavers together, I recognize the token."

" And I am sure of it, too," said Allen, as he took out his knife and began scraping off the wax covering. " Didn't I tell you so? There they are, both engraved, and as like as two peas in a pod—'Willie Williamson' on this; 'Charlie Williamson' on that."

The black must needs put his oar in, and he declared that "just as sure as de sun shines above, dey bof am alike." Negro-like, he grinned from ear to ear and clapped his hands, crowing like a rooster, of which he gave a first-rate imitation.

CHAPTER IX.

WHILE this performance was being enacted, the Indians stood staring in amazement at the scene, and Sambo fairly danced with joy, as did his friend also, full of glee as they realized the almost miraculous reunion of the brothers; while Walker looked upon the twins with a keen relish, as the captain seized the hand of his long-lost brother, and they fell on each other's neck, as did David and Jonathan, and kissed each other.

"Captain," said Allen, "it was not my fault that that likely brother of yourn didn't bite the dust, when I gave him a slight wound, for I thought he was as much an Indian as the copper-headed fellows he was leading against us."

"Yes," replied the brother, "it was a lucky escape indeed for him."

"You'd have worked daylight into or out of him, you bet?" said the darkey.

"No, Ebony; it would have been pitch-dark very soon for him, if he hadn't dodged so quickly behind the sapling."

At this moment the tall, muscular native came forward, supporting the crippled white man in disguise, who was no one else but Le Fort, who figures so conspicuously in the first part of our story.

"My dear children ! my own dear boys ! God bless you ! We are united now again at last, never, I trust, to be parted while we live."

"What !" exclaimed old Yankee Allen, "are you indeed the father of these two boys ? You know it was this old darkey and I who found them on that wrecked vessel off the shoals of Nantucket."

"And what of the mother, my dear wife ?

Do tell me at once what has become of her," gasped Le Fort.

" The beautiful woman ? Why, we laid her away at rest on old ocean's bed, to sleep the sleep that knows no waking here."

At this intelligence Le Fort bowed his head in grief, for he had hoped, now he was so happy, that his wife survived her voyage to fill his cup of joy to the full.

" Oh, this is sad indeed, to think that she was cast into the sea, and I shall never behold her sweet face again ! "

Allen seemed to have a doubt that Le Fort was the father of the two boys, now grown to manhood, and asked for proofs of the fact.

But the captain said, " Enough, my friend, if we have found a real parent, as we believe. Why cast a cloud over new-found happiness ? We are waifs from the perils of the sea, too young to know the authors of our being."

"The handsome lady was voyaging to the States to meet her husband," interrupted Sambo, " 'cause she said the two little cubs had a papa there, jest afore she breeved away her last bref."

" Well," replied Allen, " if indeed this boy is your son, he's as noble a one as ever trod the deck of a man-of-war. But who'd have thought of finding his father among wild savages ? "

Le Fort, having recovered his surprise on thus suddenly finding his sons, whom he supposed to have perished at sea with their mother, at once began to relate how it was he became separated for a while from his family, and soon all doubts were put at rest as to his being indeed the father of the twins.

He was born in France, and had a desire to emigrate to Canada, shortly after his marriage. On arriving at Quebec, he was engaged in trading for furs and peltry, and seeing a fair prospect of accumulating a fortune, he made arrangements for his wife to join him. Judge how anxiously he watched for the vessel that should bring to him his earthly treasures. But the ship was nearly lost in a storm, and the only persons saved from shipwreck were the poor wife and her two children. The ship did not founder and go down, but drifted a wreck off Nantucket shoals, where the *Dancing Feather* fell in with it, and rescued the two children.

Le Fort was his assumed name, he said, the real one being Williamson, after whom his wife had named the two boys. Not hearing any tidings of the vessel, he had made up his mind to return to his native country, and leaving Canada, he went back to Paris.

There he soon learned that the vessel had undoubtedly been lost at sea, and again he returned to America, and concluded to settle among the Hollanders on the Hudson river. He fell in with fur traders, and often acted as a scout and guide to the trappers back and forth to Canada among the French settlers.

At the time of our parties landing where he was, near Vanderheyden's landing in the North river, he got information that Van Buren's idea was to rob them if he could, and he made up his mind to thwart his plans, if possible; so he quarrelled with his companion to find out the truth of the matter.

On leaving the neighbourhood so suddenly, he overtook the party and piloted them along the Hudson to the Mohawk valley, up to Onieda Castle and on to the salt springs in Onondaga, where he came across the old chief, Thay-an-da-na-ga, who had saved his life once, and he agreed to stay with him and share his wigwam.

While sojourning here, a young Indian came in one day, and brought the news of a great slaughter by the whites, and that the adopted son of the chief was slain. But the same youth, who had been so kindly cared for and nursed in illness by Estelle, was the very one who was saved, but supposed to be lost for ever to him. The messenger who brought the news said he saw him lying dead on Fort Hill.

At once the chief set out with this young fellow as guide to the fort, some twenty-five miles away to the westward. Then it was that Estelle, Bostwick, Allen, and Bond were seized and bound, expecting soon to be slain. But the young son of the chief interceded to save them if he possibly could.

Finding only these four of the party attacked, they resolved to go forth and capture the rest of them; that is, the captain, Walker, and Sambo, the coloured man. When Walker and the captain left, with the faithful black servant, they were in search of old Griffith, but were unsuccessful; and they were returning to Fort Hill and had crossed the Owasco outlet, in sight of the fort, when the natives surrounded them and made them all prisoners. But fortunately old Griffith had heard, as he was following the trail of a bear in the forest, that some whites were captured, and he resolved to go and see who they were, and perhaps be the means of saving the lives of some strangers. Little did he dream of finding his own daughter there among them, doomed to die an ignominious and cruel death.

N

Some time before this, the foster-son of the great Onondaga chief, whom Estelle had taken such good care of, discovered that he had lost the keepsake which he always wore near his heart, and felt very sad indeed about it.

On the morning the party was brought out, this young fellow had wandered in the woods with Le Fort. The Indians thought to seize the opportunity, in the absence of the chief, to suddenly slay their prisoners, as needful to appease the spirits of their slain comrades, whose souls were waiting an entrance to the happy hunting grounds. But the providential return of Le Fort baffled their hellish designs, just as they were about to slay them with their arrows.

They had fallen in with old Griffith in their ramblings, and he at once returned with them. Time had passed away, however, and made him forget young Williamson, whom he had brought with him from the river Yantic, in Connecticut, as, soon after he had hid himself in the wilderness, the little fellow had been suddenly surprised by some wild Indians, and carried off he knew not where, and henceforth had heard nothing about him. The Chief Brant, as the English called him, had lost a son about that time, and he concluded to adopt the little fellow as his own.

Some time afterwards, Griffith, while hunting on Fort Hill, lost the silver token which he had taken from the child, and worn himself among his other Indian trappings about his neck. The story runs that he lost the medal, with strings attached, in some bushes, and when the eagles were picking up twigs with which to build a nest, they carried it up with grass and leaves to the limb of a tree, and there it remained for a long time, till found by the captain.

The captain, when he came to Fort Hill, had a spy-glass such as all navy vessels carried on the ocean; and while surveying the flocks of wild pigeons which were flying over, something glittered in the sunlight among the chestnut trees. His curiosity was awakened, and he determined to climb the tree and see what it was of so singular a nature in the wilderness. What a wonderful discovery, to be sure! It seemed something more than chance or good luck. He thought it was providential, for he discovered a missing link carrying him back to his early years. Long lost indeed, but now restored and far dearer to him than a pot of gold! On showing it to his comrade Allen, he, as well as the black, Sam, at once recognized it as belonging to one of the twin brothers.

CHAPTER X.

THE wars of the English and the French, and so, too, of the colonists along the St. Lawrence and the Hudson, are so well described in Cooper's novels, that we have no need to speak of them in detail here. The Indian tribes called the Iroquois, or Six Nations, were very much mixed up with these parties, and added greatly to the cruelties of that unholy strife of that early day.

The French general of the forces had vowed to exterminate the Six Nations, who summoned a large grand council, when war to the knife was decided on among the tribes. They were gathering all their warriors to repel the French and the Canadian Indians, who were coming against them across the St. Lawrence river.

Le Fort had learned all about this from his chief; so all the party which had gathered together on Fort Hill agreed, as the best thing they could do, to set forth towards their former home on the North river, far below Albany.

Le Fort and Walker, however, thought best to

pay a visit to a fur-trading post on the banks
of Lake Ontario.

So the twins, now united, with Walker and
Le Fort, started on their journey northward to
Oswego, leaving Estelle with old Griffith, Bond,
Allen, and the coloured man, who was good com-
pany and a safe protector.

The Indians had nearly all scattered, except a
few who were dissatisfied, and who ground their
teeth in rage that they had thus been cheated
out of a grand "pow-wow" and death of their
victims.

Yankee Allen and Sambo, now thoroughly
disgusted with Indian fighting, were not slow
to set their faces towards the rising sun.

"What would I just give to be on board the
old cruiser *Butterfly* once more," said Allen,
"with our rations of grog served up regularly
twice a day?"

"And I too, massa; and when we all jine
ag'in on de old shores of de noble Hudson,
we'll h'ist the anchor and sail away on de broad
ocean!"

"I tell you, Sam," said the other, "I don't like
the looks of these Indians, somehow. They remind me of the Evil One, ready to seek and
devour us, and when we least expect it."

"Golly, I'm of de same 'pinion, and I wonder how young missus' father kep from being killed. He must know 'em pretty well by dis time?"

They thus kept up each other's courage, as we say children do, who whistle or sing in the dark.

Allen declared that one of the Indians gave him a fierce look, just as he was about to stick a knife in him while bound to the tree, when they were timely rescued, and he was sure if the Indian got a chance, he would slake his vengeance in taking his life.

" Well, we'll keep our eyes skinned then," said the darkey, " and you no catch dis child asleep any more 'n you catch a weasel asleep!"

While this talk was going on, Estelle and her father noticed how the Indians persisted in hanging round, as if reluctant to go. Griffith said he smelled mischief brewing, and he told his daughter of it; but they were too cautious to betray themselves or show any fear.

The Indians pretended to be engaged only in a wrestling match, a trial of skill, tumbling one another upon the ground, and rolling among the dry leaves, much to the amazement of Sambo and Allen.

Sambo said he could land him on the deck if

on board of ship, pointing to the very lithe form of one of the Indians. The Indian understood the gesture, and came forward, motioning by signs that he was eager for a trial, if the black was willing.

"Try him," said the other, "and I'll bet you can tumble him over the log yonder. If you do it, I'll give you a plug of tobacco and an extra grog of New England rum."

At once they joined in locking arms, and it was difficult to tell which was proving most skilful for a while in dodging each the other's feints to throw the other, but once the Indian lifted Sambo off his feet. The black, who knew a trick or two, and what was called the knuckle, or lock-knee trick, by pushing his right knee into the Indian's left leg came near throwing his antagonist, but both fell to the ground together. This drew a loud laugh from all the Indians. This was declared even, and Sambo was ready for another trial.

"Double the reward," said his backer, "if you fetch him this time."

Now all became a scene of excitement. Sambo declared he'd make him measure his length on the ground; and at it they went again, holding each other at arm's length. They gazed into each

other's eyes for a few moments, when the tall
Indian again tried to lift Sambo off his feet; but
his move was detected, and Sambo foiled him.
He knew his enemy lacked wind, for he was
panting, and so he began to tire him out by
skirmishes, till by-and-by he made a powerful
effort and threw the Indian prone to the ground,
with so great a force as to draw from him a
groan of pain.

Allen shouted out, " Well done, old boy! you've
conquered!"

But the other Indians were mad at this defeat,
and setting up a howl, rushed at once forward
and seized the black, trying to throw him to the
ground.

There was a good reason why they had challenged the black to this conflict of skill and
strength.

CHAPTER XI.

It was plain to the whites that all this manœu-
vring on the part of the Indians meant mischief.
The red men only wanted an occasion to slake

their thirst for vengeance in the blood of their white foes, and so they made their discomfiture in the wrestling match a pretence for picking a quarrel.

The black man quickly shook himself free, but others closed in upon him. Allen, seeing that the black was holding his own and tumbling the savages one over another, loudly cheered him; but Sambo was "getting his mad up," as he called it, seeing they were disposed to pit three or four upon one. With an almost superhuman effort, he threw two of them to the ground, and drawing back a few paces, declared he would fight the whole of the crew, if they didn't let him alone.

Allen, above the savage yells of the Indians, bade them "hold off!" or he would harm some of them. He might as well have whistled to the wind, or, as one said, "have sung psalms to a dead horse!" All of them, full of anger at their disappointment, made a dash upon the black at once, determined to seize him.

"I'll stand by you," said Allen. "If they touch a lock of your wool, I will give them 'Hail, Columbia!'"

The struggle now became intense, and it seemed doubtful which would win. Allen gave a powerful Indian a blow which sent him a kiting, head over heels.　Then half a dozen sprang upon the brave man, and he had to yield, as they secured him with thongs and bound him fast. Next came the black's time, and after he had felled one or two, he was overpowered and bound likewise.

Then, in turn, came old Griffith out of the tent, agitated with fear, not for himself, but for his lovely daughter.　At once he ran in among them, and tried to calm and quiet the frenzied Indians, but he too might as well have asked the Falls of Niagara to stop their deafening roar. They, in their excitement, were deaf to all entreaty.

He turned back to where Estelle was, to see how best he could protect her.　In her fright she had fallen down in a swoon, and was deadly pale. Her father thought she was dying or dead, and he burst out in tones of lamentation, praying God to spare his dear child.

He bore her to the air, and was met at the tent door by two or three Indians howling like fiends. But the sight of the poor girl, pale and almost lifeless, made them halt; for death, or its semblance, is alike appalling to all human beings, and even animals and domestic birds are startled and moved at sight of one of their dead.* Estelle's hand was resting upon the old man's shoulder, and her long hair hung down in wavy folds, nearly to the ground, while her face was as white and transparent as Parian marble.

Not minding them, the old man was bearing his precious charge along, to bathe her head at a spring of water close by. The Indians, recovering from their surprise, at once tore her from the old man and bore her away, while they tied her father fast to the ground upon his back. As soon as they had carried their victim a few rods off, they shouted in triumph.

The men prisoners were at a loss to know what next would turn up, in the misfortune they had met with, and could only wait with patience, as best they could, for some new development. Allen said the silence was awful. " Give me anything but suspense," added he. " I wonder what next they will do ? " Each one had an opinion to give, and all concluded that the chief having gone away, they would certainly be put to death.

---

* Persons may doubt this, thinking the birds and brute creation are dumb animals and have not reasoning powers. But let any one kill a fowl or chicken by cutting off its head, and if blood is seen by the live fowls they show signs of being frightened, and set up a noise, perhaps saying one to another, " How barbarous to kill one of our family ! "

But none were braver than the darkey. He said, "I s'pose my 'pinion ain't of much account, any way! A live nigger arn't woff much; much more a dead one! They can't kill me but once, and a beating don't last long."

Strange how a little burst of humour, even in danger, seems to cheer up companions in misery. One cracked his jokes on the poor blacky, telling him that the savages might, just as likely as not, raise his hair (meaning a scalping of his wool). The chances of his escaping this painful operation were ten to one in his favour, as the Indians might, possibly, appropriate Sam to themselves, to be of service in helping them to preserve their game of dried venison for the winter. Sam said he would like to be their cook for a day or two. Not that they would appreciate his skill in getting up a good dinner; but he would like to put in some ingredients, such as wild parsnips in their broth; but they would not need any more soup, he said, this side of their happy hunting grounds.

As night drew on, they became resigned to their fate, believing that they were as well prepared to die now as at any time, and each believing also that they had done right in killing their enemies, who had tried to kill them. And thus it was they beguiled the weary hours of the the evening, and sank into a quiet repose.

CHAPTER XII.

BUT sleep, sweet as it is to the weary, was not undisturbed in the tent on Fort Hill. About midnight, Griffith started to get on his feet, at the sound of a piercing cry, but was fast tied down by the thongs which encircled his wrists and ankles. "What is that?" he exclaimed.

This roused the black out of a deep sleep, and he cried out, "Fire de Lord, de debbils are coming, sure enough!"

"Hush! you lubber," cried Allen; "it's only a panther or night owl. Indians do not slaughter their victims in the dark; they prefer the daylight, when they can see and enjoy the writhings of their dying victims."

Sambo, in his struggle to meet the "debbil," as he supposed, had succeeded in getting one of his paws loose, and asked one of his companions in trouble for a knife, so as to set himself entirely free. He put his hand into old Griffith's pocket and drew out a knife, with which he proceeded to cut the bonds of all, and set them free. The old man bade them remain perfectly quiet.

At nightfall, the Indians made a fire to cook some squirrels, and after setting a guard to watch the prisoners, they proceeded to devour their evening meal.

Let us see what had become of the frightened Estelle. After the sortie, she was separated from her friends and carried down into a glen, just where one visiting the place will find the tomb of New York's favourite son, who was a governor of the State, and afterwards a senator and member of the cabinet of the President. Here rude wigwams had been constructed by the savages, and into one of them she was conveyed.

One can hardly imagine what fearful thoughts came into her mind, as she reflected upon the chance of a cruel fate awaiting her and her father! Ah, yes! and perhaps a lover, too, was in her mind, whom she was never again to behold.

It was while thinking of her sad condition that she espied a light, and a savage approached, bearing in his hand a lighted pine-knot. He stood over her for a moment, and on her opening her eyes, he addressed her in broken English. This was a surprise indeed.

She said to him, " Have you come to kill me ? If so, pray be merciful."

" No," he said ; " I am come to save you. I am one whom chance has sent to release you and all your friends."

" Ah ! can you ? will you ? " she exclaimed, as hope now began to animate her breast.

" I can, and will, as sure as the Great Spirit lives ! "

" And my father and his companions, too ? "

" All but one," he replied. " The council have decided that one of them must die. He has slain so many of the red men that his life is forfeit ; he cannot escape."

She knew at once whom he meant—it was Bond.

" The good Lord be with him ! " she ejaculated. " But why cannot you save him, if you will ? He slew others only in self-defence."

" You know not the laws of Indian warfare," he replied.

" Sure, he will be saved. It is hard to die here in the wilderness, and be buried far from kindred and friends."

" I cannot answer that," said he.

Estelle resolved that she, too, must die, if her father must end his days. And the savage, seeing how sorrowful she looked, said he would do all in his power for her, and then left the wigwam.

The night passed away, while hope and fear alternated in her mind; at length daylight appeared. Of the rest, none had slept more soundly than Bond—the most to be pitied of all ; for he had made up his mind, he said, " to die game."

Soon all were startled by a loud outcry of the natives. Something had happened, but they knew not what it was. The old man looked, and saw something was engaging them besides their prisoners. It was evident that the Indians were preparing for an attack from some foes outside the fort.

Sambo was the first to discover the barking of a dog, and he knew it meant something ominous. " Do you hear that, massa ? " said he.

" Yes," one replied ; " that's old Bose, sure as you live." Another, " That's the captain's dog— they have returned."

All at once the savages rushed into the tent, with tomahawks and knives uplifted to slay their prisoners. They had expected to find their prisoners fast bound, as they had left them; but suddenly they all rose to their feet, and one seized a pole close at hand, with which he kept them at bay. Realizing that the French had attacked the savages outside, they saw hope dawning upon them once more, if they could defend themselves till rescued. The black, with a club, knocked over one Indian, and seizing his tomahawk, made quick work in despatching him.

The natives, thus baffled, had to beat a sudden retreat; and at once in rushed a lot of armed men, led on by Le Fort, Walker, and the twin brothers, who had arrived just in the nick of time to save them.

CHAPTER XIII.

THE sudden delivery from the very jaws of death is what few experience in life where such dangers threaten, especially on battle-fields or far away from civilization. All were suddenly raised from the depths of despair to a longer lease of life; and, let us hope, their hearts beat lively, if their lips did not express it, with gratitude to "the Giver of every good and perfect gift" for their safety.

It was said that the darkey indulged in quite an eloquent oration over the dead form of the savage whom he had slain. He said, " You was mighty 'cute, old *Injun*, now warn't you, comin' in here widout knocking, into our sleepin' apartments ? Perhaps, old fellow, your mother never tole you, 'First catch your fish afore you cooks 'em !' Nebber mind, old chap, I'll gib you a decent funeral; and mebbe de crows'll come and sing a hymn ober your grave." Sam had heard, evidently, of the old story of " Cock Robin," where one of the birds promised to be "the parson," but wasn't a crow by any means. Then he gave a kick at the Indian's shins in perfect disgust.

The scenes here recorded were of only a few moments' duration, but how all was changed for them ! It often takes longer to tell of a battle than it does to fight it.

It must not be supposed that the twin brothers were long in asking after Estelle. Both in one breath demanded of Griffith where she was. " The good Lord only knows," were all the words he could utter. But recovering, he added, " The savages rose upon us yesterday, and we had to submit. They carried off my child, and she may be dead for aught I know."

"Which way went they ? " asked the captain, while his brother ran out of the tent the way the Indians had retreated.

"There's no use chasing them," said Allen ; "they're miles away by this time towards the Cayuga."

The unfortunate girl had gotten into a quiet repose, when she heard the yells of the demon savages outside her cabin door. She had just time to rise, when five or six rushed in, still howling, and at the sight of them she fell in a swoon upon the ground, feeling that now her time had come. When she came to, she found that she was being carried away by the young Indian who had visited her on the previous evening and promised to save her.

"Alas ! " she exclaimed, "where am I ? "

"Safe with one who will not harm you ; not a hair of your head."

"But father—where is he ? "

"Safe. They are all gone—fled far away."

Soon she heard footsteps approaching, and she gladly beheld the form of the twin brother Charlie. Then she knelt on one knee, and thanked the

good Lord for her deliverance from the very
jaws of death.

Charlie rapidly informed her of himself and
party; how they had met some French soldiers,
and how they had scattered the Indians in time
to save her father and all, with the black man.
No wonder her heart beat with lively emotions
on beholding him whose life she had saved.

They soon retraced their steps to the fort, where
they were surrounded by the released prisoners,
Le Fort, her father, and the rest of them. Here
was a new revelation as the party met. It goes
back to our first chapter.

"My eyes!" exclaimed Le Fort, "Diedrich,
you here! Where, in the name of all that's
good, did you come from?"

"Why, of course, from the Hudson river. Where
else could I come from? Dick Van Buren is
dead—your enemy, who hated you so, and would
have killed you most certainly—was drowned
while trying to swim across the Mohawk.
Chance has brought me here to save the life
of this young lady, who is a real angel."

Le Fort looked upon his twin boys with a
manly pride, as he thought how mercifully they
had been rescued from a watery grave.

The query of the black man was put to the

leader, as to their exodus out of the wilderness into "the Lord's Country," as he called civilization in the eastern part of New York.

After a hearty supper on venison, trout fresh from the lake, and good coffee, a council was held, and the captain said the next morning, bright and early, they would set their faces homeward. At sound of these stirring words, Sambo threw a somersault and danced as he never did before, declaring he was never so happy in his life.

That night they all slept as sound as roaches, nothing being near to make them afraid.

CHAPTER XIV.

THE dangers to which Estelle had been exposed, added to the fatigue she had borne, were enough to make her look old and drive away the rose colour of her cheeks. For it has often happened that men and women have had their hair turn almost white in a few hours through a great sorrow or sudden fear. But though her features were assuming a womanly touch, she looked, in the eyes of that party, as a queen of beauty, for all admired her, while at least one must have her. Perhaps it was one of the twin brothers? We shall see. Her father, too, was justly proud of her, and looked with pride upon the twin brothers, as they both seemed to vie with each other in paying her every attention.

Among the French party who came in time to release the prisoners was a French officer named La Valliet; he too became a suitor of the fair American girl. This is a habit with a good many gallant Frenchmen, who manage to fall in love with our beautiful countrywomen, declaring that none in the world can surpass the handsome American girls. There was an excuse, too, for it was novel and romantic to find one so gifted in mind and beautiful in appearance as Estelle, who might have been compared to a rose in the desert. The French officer declared she was as pretty as a fairy, and that he adored her. He had seen belles and women in Paris in ball-rooms and at parties; but here she shone brightly among nature's charms, and that, too, with little beside nature's adorning. He was continually speaking of her as a floral gem that would shine in Paris, at the French court, if transplanted on French soil. But he was cautioned to beware how he let his affections become entangled, as one of the young Americo-French twins, whose life she had saved in the forest, was her favoured suitor. But, French-like, he could not imagine that a tawny young man, habited in Indian costume of buckskin and leggings, could stand any chance with him if he urged his suit. Then he became jealous, and resolved he would win her in spite of any one.

Le Fort and his friends had made up their minds, as stated, to begin their journey before the French should commence their great battle with the Indians, for this might delay their journey eastward.

It was known that the Indians had been gathering at Onondaga Hill to attack the French, and they chose Fort Hill as a safe defence to abide in and await an attack from the Onondagas and Cayugas. They, however, provided an escort of a few armed men, under La Valliet, which soon set out, skirting the shore of the Skaneatedes Lake. Thus they could reconnoitre the position of the Indians, and report to their commander; and thus he had opportunities which he could avail himself of to let Estelle know how violently he was in love with her.

La Valliet told the twin brothers of the commission committed to him, and how he was
willing to be the escort of the party. They
replied that they were obliged to him indeed,
but they really feared no danger. But he was
determined to go in the same direction, and
they could not well get rid of him.

The first halt in their journey was at the salt
springs. Charlie was consulted by the Frenchman as to his knowledge of the various tribes
he had met. He bore testimony to the courage,
bravery, and skill of all the tribes of the Six
Nations among whom he had visited, and he prophesied long and cruel warfare before they could
be subdued, if at all. But La Valliet thought
that this caution reflected upon the valour of
the French, imagining the savages to be only
brutes, with instincts, but hardly gifted with
reasoning faculties. He even went so far as to
call his companion a half-civilized person. The
youth flashed a look of indignation in return
for this insult, and felt tempted to draw his
knife; but he kept cool, saying, " Perhaps you
had better try me."

This sudden outburst of passion startled the
rest of the officers, as the young man moved
away.

" Ah," said the Frenchman, " you no get off in that way. I shall chastise you, I shall."

The reply he got was this : " You call yourselves the Grand Nation. If you want my opinion of an average Frenchman, I'd say he's a cross between a tiger and a monkey ; so put that in your pipe and smoke it, if you like."

The Frenchman had fought duels at home, and his rank would suffer in reputation if he did not resent an insult, even from a civilian. All this trouble was the effect of bad temper, added to La Valliet's fit of jealousy.

Charlie did not think he would show any pluck, but he was mistaken, for La Valliet at once followed him—to " settle their hash," as Sambo called it.

CHAPTER XV.

NED had not gone far from the presence of the French commander, when he met old Allen, the sailor, and at once informed him that a storm was brewing between himself and the French captain, who now came up and demanded what he wanted. At this Allen spoke up and said, "Perhaps my room here is better than my company?"

"No," replied his friend. "This fellow has used language personally insulting to myself, and he must retract it."

"Hold!" said Allen, turning to the Frenchman, "I rescued this boy from a watery grave, and I'll see fair play, you may depend upon it."

"I do not know you, sir," said the Frenchman. "Who are you?"

"Well, I am an old salt, a tar, if you want to know, and can pitch such chaps as you into the middle of next week, if occasion should offer. I'd like to know who *you* are?"

"Sir," said he, drawing himself up, "I serve the King of France, and I find it necessary to chastise some of these Americans, who have no royal blood in them."

"Ho, ho!" replied the tar, "here's a go. I happened to be at the battle of Tripoli and Algiers, and the way I laid the cat-o'-nine tails over those refractory Turks couldn't be beat. Besides, I've whipped a live catamount—chased a black bear through the woods, and when the old customer got on top of a log, I caught him by the tail, till he growled at me and I let him go. I was with

General Putnam when he stole two cubs from that cave and made a successful retreat."

While this parley was going on, the rest of the officers, with Le Fort, father of the youth insulted, drew near, and demanded what it all meant.

La Valliet seemed to wish to avoid his companions, and speaking a few words in a low tone, walked off, followed by Charlie.

The officers who remained with Charlie's friends said to William (the captain twin brother), " Blood will have to be shed, according to our French code of honour, for your brother's language was very irritating."

" Well, so be it," replied the other; " my brother is plucky and will not shirk the consequences."

" If he should," said Allen, " I am an old seaman and will take his place."

" Never mind," said the captain. " I'll answer for him ; he's not a drop of a coward's blood in his whole skin."

Le Fort, feeling all a parent's anxiety, was bent on interfering, for he loved his new-found son too well to run any risk of losing him. So he rushed forward, followed by the darkey, and they soon heard the sound of blows at a short distance from them. Sam was the first to find the couple, and he stopped short on beholding them, as they were fighting desperately.

The black cheered his master on, and was more than half inclined to have a hand in himself, but that would never do. It seemed as though one or both must die, as their knives glittered in the light of the moon.

Le Fort rushed forward as though he would stand between them, but they were too close together, and he demanded of them to desist. But it was too late; La Valliet had received a wound, and fell as if lifeless to the earth.

Then Estelle, having an inkling of what was going on, came upon the scene, just as the French officer fell, when she saw that her lover was also wounded, and at sight of his blood fell down in a fainting fit.

The companions of La Valliet soon gathered some sticks, formed a litter, and bore him away to their quarters.

Ned was not badly wounded—only some cuts on his arms which would be scars for life in what he called " an honourable warfare."

On the other hand, Allen and the black were exultant, showing their approval in an amusing way, because their side had triumphed.

"Cuffee!" said Allen, "what do you think of our brave boy? He hasn't shown the white feather, as Mons. Crapeau thought he would, eh?"

"Not much," replied the ebony sailor, as he showed his white ivory teeth, grinning like a "Cheshire cat." "Gorra, massa, how he did let daylight into him! He no more eat frog's legs for he supper."

But let us not be too cruel. He was in love with Estelle and may be pardoned for picking a quarrel. We all know how many great wars have grown out of the troubles in which women have had a hand. The spilling of a glass of wine on a queen's dress caused a war of great magnitude; and to the Empress Eugénie is attributed Napoleon's declaring war with Germany.

The surgeon who belonged to the expedition carefully examined the wounds and dressed them. All, even the Americans, were glad to learn that they would not prove fatal.

The next day, it was agreed, was to be their last in the Far West, and so they retired early to their bivouac fires, to start with the early dawn.

CHAPTER XVI.

At midnight Griffith awoke and took a look out of the door of the tent where his dear child Estelle was sleeping. He saw the two sentinels meet on their rounds and cry, "All's well!" From the head-quarters of the commander he could see a light burning, for La Valliet was lying in a feverish state, cursing now and then "the Yankee," as if his mind was still dwelling on the awful conflict. Griffith's tent was only a few rods from the place where others of the party had sought shelter under an old Indian *wiekup*. He carefully looked into it to see if all was as it should be. He found Allen and the black man wide awake and spinning yarns of olden times on the Hudson.

By-and-by Sambo started up and exclaimed, "What dat dur? Massa, didn't you hear a noise?"

"No; all I hear is a tree-toad, which always makes that noise when it's going to rain. I did hear a whip-poor-will a few moments ago."

All of a sudden, the reports of two pistols were

heard near the French camp, and this was followed as usual by those yells which, once heard from savage throats, can never be mistaken or forgotten. It is the cry of fell revenge, and means death without mercy. The Indians were almost as thick as leaves, as Sambo said; they seemed to swarm like bees around the French, after picking off the sentinels, so near, and yet no previous alarm had been given of their approach.

The wily savages had adopted a new plan to pick off the sentinels. In the woods were wild hogs running about, and the Indians and whites were glad to hunt and kill them for a good roast. Well, two of the Indians, in the darkness which followed when the moon passed under a cloud, crawled up softly and stealthily among the leaves, on their bellies, quite up to the guards, grunting like the pigs, and thus deceived them! The soldiers rushed out of their shelter, and, in the confusion of the moment, many of them were slain by the infuriated savages. The war-paint on their faces indicated a determination to exterminate their foes.

The French had gone to their slumbers little dreaming of what awaited them. They supposed in a year, or maybe a less time, they could conquer the refractory Indians, and be recalled to *la belle France* with honours won in battle, and meet again their beloved friends and relatives in their home of the vine and the olive! But, alas! none of them were ever to hear again the sweet voices of little children, or the hum of the spinning-wheel, found everywhere in the homes of the peasantry; for their bones were to lie bleaching on the soil of a foreign land, or be buried far from all they held dear in life!

Of course the light in the tent of the wounded Le Valliet first drew their attention, and thither they wended their steps. The watcher, who was standing at the head of the prostrate officer, was the first to be despatched; and as one of the savages, who was the first to enter, threw a tomahawk at La Valliet, he discharged his two pistols at the heads of the two nearest him; and these were the sounds which were heard by Griffith and the others.

The French soldiers, as soon as they could recover from the panic into which they had been thrown, at once rallied, and a deadly warfare began. For a long time the Indians seemed to be on the point of success. Anon they would give way under the galling fire of the old cavalry or horse pistols of the French, who used their sabres too with a deadly effect. The temporary shelters of the soldiers were no barriers to protect them, so the fight became a dreadful hand-to-hand encounter, causing blood to flow on every side. The moon broke forth in a full blaze, and thus gave light to distinguish friend from foe. The orders of the French commander rang out clear, and he animated his soldiers with the cry, " Down with the villains ! Death to every savage ! "

As we may imagine, the quarters of Estelle and her party were close by, and they were soon aware of the dangers surrounding them. A hurried consultation was held as to what was best to be done. But they too were soon discovered, and the rascals, maddened by blood, were only bent on shedding that of every white, friend or foe.

The first to meet the savage who rushed toward them was Sambo, who caught the Indian round his waist, and lifting him off his feet, threw him upon the ground with a violence that stunned him ; then, jumping upon him, drove his breath clean out of his body.

This daring feat of the black hero nerved Allen to pitch in also, and see how many he could lay low. He struck out right and left, felling

P

many a savage to the ground. But just as he had fought and overcome a brave warrior, another Indian came up behind him and struck him on the head with a tomahawk, causing him to fall and die without a struggle.

This was a sad sight for poor black Sam, who had, with him, sailed across the Spanish main, fighting pirates and always victorious together. But to be cut down by brutes was too much for the poor fellow to behold without stirring his heart deeply in sympathy for his old comrade, whose voice he never more would hear upon the earth. Dropping a few tears over his fallen friend, he roused himself, bent on revenging him who could not revenge himself, though his own brave right arm was hanging by his side, powerless.

The warfare had now raged at least half an hour, the whole body of whites were completely surrounded, and the savages had the advantages mostly on their side in the hand-to-hand encounter. At a distance, the soldiers were sure to win, as their rifles were more than a match for the Indians' weapons of bows and arrows, knives and tomahawks.

The American captain looked for his brother, whom he had missed in the general fray. Meeting Sambo, he saw him ready to pounce upon the slayer of his companion. With an iron grasp Sambo seized the wretch, and each gave the other a deadly blow, both falling at the same time to rise no more.

All at once the whole scene changed. The tall chief, who commanded the Indians, appeared with the twin brother upon the scene. The loud voice of Thay-an-da-na-ga was heard bidding a parley. This the savages obeyed. They knew not what it meant, but none dared disobey the voice of the chief.

We all know that one of the twins had been the adopted son of the chief, and he had sought and found him in time to reach the scene of the strife, and thus save Estelle, her father, and all except poor Allen and Sambo, who had lived and died together, brave and noble and deeply lamented.

TO CONCLUDE.

As the sun rolled up next morning, as big as a great cart-wheel, shining down upon that bloody battle-field, it filled them all with horror. The natives were the conquerors, for not a solitary soldier was left to tell the tale.

Our friends, however, were seen, or might have

been seen, threading their way through the forests and over the hills of the Onondaga and Oneida, where no woodman's axe had yet been heard, and the stillness of the wild woods was unbroken, save by the cry of the whip-poor-will, the eagle, the hawk, or wild heron, or the more terrible howling of wild beasts in search of prey.

To-day, the same scene shows the progress of religion and civilization, where the cattle graze upon a thousand hills, and where are homes filled with hearts and hands of children of those noble pioneers, who were the hardy settlers of the early day. Then all was toil and struggle with poverty and self-denial to reclaim the wilderness and make it blossom as the rose.

After a solemn committal to the earth of Allen and the faithful African, the party took their leave, never to return.

A few years later, a lovely farmhouse, with barns full, and stacks of hay, and with flocks and herds surrounding, could be seen on the banks of Connecticut river, and close by the farmhouse and dairy was an

"Old oaken bucket, the iron-bound bucket,
The moss-covered bucket, which hung in the well."

A double wedding was celebrated at the nuptials of Estelle and her twin lover; while the other, the handsome captain, had somehow found a charming mate among New England's fair daughters, who had consented to be a party to make complete the happiness of our heroes, the Jacob and Esau of modern times.

Whoever has been a guest of the olden time, not too proud to eat in a New England kitchen, will readily recall the surroundings of a New England wedding. Cake and cider, baked pork and beans, old fashioned dough-nuts and crullers, homely as we may regard them, were then necessary adjuncts of every entertainment where festive joy reigned.

What the future life of Estelle was we cannot tell. But it was said by an old lady that " she and her husband lived in peace, and died full of honours, leaving a noble lot of boys and girls, some of whom became ministers and lawyers and doctors, and the females were the mothers of governors and statesmen."

The writer ranks himself among them.

APPENDIX.

I.

PAUL JONES'S GREAT VICTORY.

THIS remarkable man's name was simply John Paul, that of Jones having been assumed in after-life for some unknown reason. At the age of twelve he was apprenticed to a merchant of Whitehaven who was engaged in the American trade. His first voyage was to Virginia, where his elder brother was established as a planter. Some time after, we hear of him as engaged in the slave-trade, but this he abandoned in disgust. Subsequently he made several voyages to the West Indies, and, it is said, accumulated a fortune by his successful speculations.

At the commencement of the Revolution Jones offered his services to the United States Government, and received a commission as lieutenant in the navy, December 22, 1775. For a time he served in a subordinate capacity, but his ability and daring became so conspicuous that within ten months he was placed in command of an expedition consisting of two vessels, the *Alfred* and the *Providence*. For the next three years we hear of him in all parts of the Atlantic coast and on the shores of Scotland, where he harassed the coasting trade, and also made a most daring and successful descent upon the town of Whitehaven.

In 1779 an important expedition was fitted out under the joint auspices of the King of France and the American Commissioners, and placed under the command of Jones. The squadron consisted of five vessels; and though four of them were French, they were to be considered as American ships, to be governed by the rules of the American navy during the cruise. The commissions of the officers were given by Dr. Franklin; and before the expedition sailed, the name of the *Duras*, Jones's flag-ship, was changed to that of *Bonhomme Richard*, as a compliment to the great philosopher. His crew of 375 men was a medley made up of representatives of almost every nation in Europe, and even Malays. The ship herself was an indifferent vessel, and equipped in a very inefficient manner. On her main or gun deck she mounted twenty-eight twelve-pounders, and on her quarter-deck and forecastle fourteen nine-pounders, making an armament of forty-two guns in all. Dissatisfied with this, Jones caused twelve ports to be cut in the room below, where six old eighteen-pounders were mounted. This expedient, however, did not add to the efficiency of the ship, but, on the contrary, produced the most disastrous consequences.

At the close of July, Jones sailed from L'Orient, on the coast of France, steered for the western shores of Ireland, and appeared off Kerry. From thence he ranged round the north of Scotland until he came opposite the Frith of Forth, when he directed his course toward Flamborough Head. By the middle of September twenty-six vessels had been captured or destroyed by the squadron, and very great alarm created upon the east coast of England. On the 23rd of the same month Jones fell in with the fleet from the Baltic, under the protection of the *Serapis*, commanded by Captain Pearson, and the *Countess of Scarborough*, commanded by Captain Piercy. Before noon Captain Pearson received intelligence from the bailiffs of Scarborough of the squadron under Jones being on the coast, and between twelve and one the enemies were in each other's sight. Signal for general chase was made by Jones, and the ship *Alliance,* being the fastest of the squadron, took the lead. Owing, however, to the cowardice or mutinous spirit of her commander, Captain Landais, on seeing the strength of the English fleet she immediately stood off at a safe distance. About half-past seven in the evening the *Richard* came up with the *Serapis,* and closed with her upon her quarter-deck to about half pistol-shot. The weather was serene and beautiful, the water perfectly smooth, and the wind light at south-west, both ships heading to the northward. It was also full moon, and Flamborough Head less than a league distant, so that the piers of Scarborough were covered with spectators eager to witness the combat. The *Serapis* now hailed the *Richard,* and was answered. A few unimportant questions passed, when broadsides were exchanged, and two of the old eighteen-pounders in the *Richard's* gun-room burst, blowing up the deck above, and killing or wounding a number of the men stationed at them. This part of the battery was then abandoned, and the ports closed. A close and heavy cannonade was now maintained by both ships for about an hour, when they fouled each other, and for a few moments the fighting ceased. Captain Pearson then hailed the *Richard,* and asked if she had struck her colours. "I have not yet begun to fight," was the reply of Jones, and the action was immediately renewed.

Captain Pearson's vessel had considerable superiority over the *Richard* in regard to her working power, and repeatedly gained advantages, in spite of the efforts of Jones to prevent it. Finally, to put an end to this, Jones aimed at laying his ship athwart of the other. Though he did not succeed in his wish, yet, as the bowsprit of the *Serapis* ran between his poop and mizzenmast, he seized the opportunity of lashing the two vessels together ; and the wind driving the head of the English ship against the bow of the *Richard,* they came so close fore and aft that the muzzles of their guns touched each other's sides.

In this position the action continued from half-past eight until half-past ten in the evening, each party fighting with the utmost desperation. As the conflict waxed warmer, they fought hand to hand with pike, pistol, and cutlass, and blood flowed freely. Already the *Richard* had been pierced by several eighteen-pound balls between wind and water; her twelve-pounders had been silenced, and she was commencing to fill. Only three nine-pounders kept up a cannonade; but the marines in the round-top sent volleys of bullets with deadly aim down upon the struggling Englishmen. Ignited combustibles were scattered over the *Serapis*, and at one time she was on fire in a dozen places. The *Serapis* also suffered much from the guns of the *Alliance*, which came up from her position of safety and deliberately poured forth her volleys indiscriminately on friend and foe. About ten o'clock the cry was raised on board the *Richard* that she was beginning to sink, and her carpenter released over a hundred prisoners, a part of whom succeeded in getting aboard the *Serapis*. The gunner also, alarmed at the quantity of water in the vessel, ran aft on the poop, crying for quarter. He was abruptly silenced by Jones. But the situation of the *Richard* was apparently hopeless. She was almost in a sinking condition, many of her guns were disabled, a large number of her prisoners were at large, the *Alliance* was deliberately firing into her, and some of the petty officers had set up the cry of fire.

Jones was advised to surrender, but repudiated the thought. The prisoners were compelled to work at the pumps, the three surviving guns kept up their fire, and the action was continued under Jones's personal super-intendence. At length the *Serapis*, overcome with the fury of her enemy, surrendered. Captain Pearson, who had nailed his flag to the mast, became convinced of the folly of prolonging the engagement, and struck his colours with his own hand. When the moment came for the gallant Englishman to deliver his sword to Commodore Jones, whom he regarded as a rebel and a pirate, it is related that he said, "I cannot, sir, but feel much mortification at the idea of surrendering my sword to a man who has fought me with a rope around his neck." Jones received the weapon, and immediately returning it, said, "You have fought gallantly, sir, and I hope your king will give you a better ship." Captain Pearson was afterward knighted as a reward for his conduct on the occasion. The story is told that, upon hearing of the event, Jones remarked, "He deserves it; and if I fall in with him again, I will make a lord of him."

Both the *Serapis* and the *Richard* had suffered much during the engagement, but the latter was a complete wreck, and the seven feet of water which she had in her hold upon the conclusion of the combat kept constantly increasing. She was on fire in two places, her quarters on the lower deck were driven in, the whole of her main battery was dismounted, and she was cut to pieces in the most extraordinary manner. The after-part of the ship, in line with the guns of the *Serapis*, was so completely demolished that the upper deck was only sustained by the ruins of the framework, some parts of which had been missed by the shot. It being considered impossible to convey her into port, the wounded were removed to the *Serapis*, and, after a short attempt to keep her afloat by means of the pumps, she was allowed to go down in the deep waters off Bridlington Bay. Commodore Jones, with the remains of his flying squadron and prizes, made for Holland, and on the 3rd of October anchored off the Texel. The prizes taken and ransomed by the *Bonhomme Richard* during her cruise were estimated at the sum of £40,000.

Upon the arrival of Jones at Holland, the British

minister at the Hague applied to the States-General for an order delivering up the *Serapis* and *Scarborough*, the latter having surrendered at the same time as the *Serapis*, together with Jones and his men. Happily the Dutch authorities refused to interfere, for they felt a secret friendship for the struggling Americans. By a diplomatic trick they also avoided trouble with Great Britain, and Commodore Jones, instead of being conveyed as a pirate to England, was soon upon the ocean as commander of the *Alliance*, the captain of that vessel having been dismissed the service on account of his conduct during the famous combat. Jones's action with the *Serapis* gave him great *éclat* in Europe and America, and no subsequent action ever dimmed his fame. Louis XVI. gave him a gold-mounted sword, bearing upon its blade the words : *Vindicati maris Ludovicus XVI., remunerator strenuo vindici.* This inscription was surrounded by the emblems of America and France. Louis also created him Knight of the Order of Merit. In 1781 he sailed for America, and here further honours were heaped upon him. General Washington wrote him an exceedingly complimentary letter, and Congress gave him a special vote of thanks. Eight years later, the same body ordered a gold medal to be struck and presented to the " Chevalier John Paul Jones." One side bore a portrait of the hero, and the other a view of the engagement by which his fame was won.

At the close of the war, Jones sailed for France, empowered to negotiate for the recovery of prize-money in different parts of Europe. This service rendered, he accepted the position of rear-admiral in the Russian navy, and on the occasion of a difficulty between that power and the Turks, acquitted himself in such a manner that he received from the Empress Catherine the ribbon of St. Anne. He was disappointed, however, in not obtaining the command of the fleet in the Black

Sea, and a quarrel with the admiral, Prince Nassau, brought him into such disgrace at court that he retired from the Russian service. A pension was promised from the Russian Government, but it was never paid, and the great naval commander retired to Paris, where he lived in poverty and neglect. His death occurred on the 18th of July, 1792, but the place of his burial is unknown. A commission from the American Government, appointing him agent to treat with Algiers, arrived too late to find him among the living.

II.

DAVY CROCKETT.

A SKETCH OF HIS LIFE—HIS ADVENTURES WITH INDIANS, AND GREAT REPUTATION AS A BEAR-HUNTER—HIS ACTS IN CONGRESS.

DAVY CROCKETT was a self-made man ; and although his example cannot be followed by our American youth, because no such circumstances can possibly arise in our history as those which attended his birth, youth, and manhood, yet still boys may learn from his example that our best and most enterprising men have had little to favour their rise in the world, and much to hinder their advancement.

An old saying is current in our literature, which originated with our hero—

" Be sure you're right, and then go ahead ! "

David Crockett, of East Tennessee, was a nondescript of human nature—neither civilized nor savage. Like Boone, Kenton, Sam Dale, etc., he was a man of circumstances. Had he lived in polished society, he would have been a popular man of the world. Brought up in the settlements strung along the Southern Indian border, he was a popular man of the woods.

Davy was the fifth child, of six sons and three daughters. His father, half squatter, half settler, led the restless life of his class, trying his hand at a dozen things and succeeding in none. The children constituted a loving family, nevertheless—sure evidence that the mother was a loving woman. Though rude and uncultivated, they were honest and true, which is more than can be said of many families who sport an escutcheon.

Davy, at an early date, had to "do" for himself. Born about 1780, he was yet a lad when the first Creek war desolated the Tennessee settlements. Then his grandparents were both butchered in their cabin home by the Indians, who had been badly treated by the whites in the neighbourhood. His uncle Joseph was wounded, and his uncle James, a mute, was carried off a prisoner, to be recovered seventeen years afterwards.

Such were the boy's early recollections. He soon became familiar with forest life, but grew up at the settlements, labouring at whatever offered for an honest living, farming, droving, teaming, etc. He ran away from his home to escape a severe whipping for refusal to go to school. Then came his first real tussle with the world, and a "rough and tumble" it was, such as boys nowadays know but little of, or such as, if they had to go through it, would leave them bad habits and broken characters.

When the second Creek war broke out in 1818, David was a married man, having two sons; but he soon enlisted, and won fame as a scout. In the several battles of the war he participated, fighting with the heroism and skill of the true borderman. But he tired of the service, of its dreadful marches and short supplies of everything needful, and returned home, near the war's close, fully satisfied to "have no more of sich doin's."

Crockett's extraordinary political career may be said to have commenced with his election to the colonelcy of a militia regiment in Giles county, where he then had "stuck his stakes."

Davy was popular, apparently, because he was ignorant; he was one of "the people," and this popularity soon sent him to the Legislature (1822), a member from Giles and Hickman counties. His ignorance was such that he did not know what the word "judiciary" meant.

A "great fresh" made Crockett a poor man by washing away his mills. He gave up everything to his creditors, and moved into the wilderness of North-west Tennessee, on the Ohio river. In that game-haunted region he spent the happiest years of his life. The woods and breaks were full of "meat," and there occurred the numerous adventures with bears which rendered Crockett famous as a hunter of ugly beasts.

But even in that wilderness the man's own political popularity followed him, and, in spite of himself, he was nominated (1823) by the people who had gathered at the little town of Jackson, forty miles away from his past home. This nomination was, by the three opposing candidates, regarded as a burlesque; but Davy, leaving his retiracy, went into the canvass so earnestly that he was elected. His remarkable speeches and odd sayings, and his great reputation as a bear-hunter, all told so powerfully in his favour that his more intelligent competitors were "nowhar."

Crockett was now a public man. His popularity was not lessened by his two winters in the Legislature, where his hunter's garb, his queer talk, and his downright honesty made him conspicuous. It is not surprising, therefore, that he should have turned his face toward Washington, by running for Congress in 1824.

Q

He was beaten, however, by two votes only, by his rich and influential opponent, the then Congress man.

He resolved to "pick his flint and try it again," after two years, when election time came on once more. During that two years he hunted much of the time. In this perilous pastime he found his greatest enjoyment as well as profit, for the meat constituted the family's main reliance for food, while the skins and oil were sold for money with which to purchase "store stuff." The stories of these prolonged hunts are exciting enough. His skill, courage, and power of endurance made him more than a match for the ferocious brutes, many of which weighed over 600 pounds each. In one year's time (1824–25) he killed 105 bears.

Davy had to give over his bear-hunting, however. In the summer of 1827 he contested the canvass for Congress against his old competitor and a wealthy and influential citizen, beating both by a large majority.

His early Congressional career was marked by devotion to the "Jackson party's" interests and principles, but never would he sacrifice his sturdy independence at the behest of his politicians. He was re-elected in 1829 by an overwhelming vote. But, during his second term, he sternly set his face against Jackson's Indian bill, as it was called, and this secured his defeat in the canvass of 1831 by a very small majority. His third canvass taught him what a dirty thing politics is—tainting every man's moral nature (if he has any moral nature to taint) who becomes a tool of political tricksters or an office-hunter.

A fourth canvass, in 1833, resulted in a dead set being made against him by the Jackson men. Jackson then literally owned the Tennessee Legislature ; so, to kill off Crockett, the Legislature re-districted the State, but all to no purpose. Davy's extraordinary popularity carried him over all intrigue and money, and he took his seat in the session of 1833–34, a strong, because wholly unfettered, man.

Despite his early ignorance, Crockett became a power as a man. He was shrewd, intelligent by nature, full of ready wit, which he used like a weapon, studious to get at the merits of every question, and perfectly fearless in expressing his convictions or wishes.

This independence, in those days of intense partisanship and detestable corruption, was so rare a virtue as to render him doubly noted ; and when, in the spring of 1834, he made his well-remembered " Northern Tour," he had a " real triumphal procession tugging on behind all the way." His reception on that tour by the Whigs of Philadelphia, New York, Boston, etc., reads like an odd romance. Everywhere thousands of people turned out to see and hear the great hunter. It was an ovation of which the honest backwoodsman was justly proud. His speeches and stories became the " town's talk," and were copied in every paper in the land. Crockett's joke-books and almanacks were immensely popular for years after.

In the closely and peculiarly contested canvass for Congress in 1835, Crockett was beaten, the Jackson party leaving no artifice or dodge untried which could impair his popularity. He was beaten by fraud, now very openly used. This defeat greatly mortified Colonel Crockett, and disgusted with politics, and broken in fortune by his long inattention to his own private affairs, he resolved to leave Tennessee altogether, and strike for Texas, whose struggles for independence were then enlisting the sympathies of the United States. Rejected by his own State, he could yet command glory in a higher and a nobler cause. It was a resolve worthy of a noble soul. Alas ! that Santa Anna's blood-dyed hands had the power to drive to butchery such a hero.

Bidding adieu to his many friends, and tearing himself from the embraces of wife and children, whom he loved with all the tenderness of his soul, he started (October, 1835) overland for San Antonio. His journey was long and exciting, full of the strangest episodes and adventures. As related in his remarkable autobiography, it reads like the invention of a romance writer. He finally reached the Texas garrison of the Alamo, at Bexar, on the San Antonio river, where the brave Colonel Travis and the renowned Colonel Bowie were awaiting the assault of Santa Anna's army, 1600 strong, then coming to redeem the defeats of General Cos, from whom San Antonio and the fortress called the Alamo had been wrenched by the Texan patriots (December 10.)

This force, under immediate command of Santa Anna, reached the vicinity of Bexar late in February, 1839, when a series of bloody struggles followed, until at last the heroic Texans were wholly driven into the works. The Alamo was assaulted on the morning of March 6th, and when finally captured, only six of the garrison of 150 were left alive, Crockett one of that number. "He stood alone in the angle of the fort, the barrel of his shattered rifle in his right hand ; in his left his large bowie-knife, dripping blood. He had a frightful gash across his forehead, while around him were a complete barrier of twenty Mexicans, lying pell-mell, dead and dying."

An appalling sight truly, but one made more appalling by the scene which soon followed—the slaughter of the six living men by Santa Anna's orders. Crockett and his companions, having surrendered as prisoners of war to General Castrillon, were led to Santa Anna, who at once ordered them to be put to the sword. "Colonel Crockett, seeing the act of treachery, instantly sprang like a tiger at the ruffian chief ; but, before he could reach him, a dozen swords were sheathed in his indomitable heart, and he fell and died without a groan, a frown on h.s brow and a smile of scorn and defiance on his lips."

Out of such scenes of carnage and martyrdom did

Texas finally emerge into the glory of independence. She truly owes a monument to these grand souls who perished in her cause ; and to none more than to the chivalric David Crockett.

III.

FALL OF THE ALAMO,

SAN ANTONIO, TEXAS.

THE fall of the Alamo, whose tragic results are so well known, was an action whose details, so far as the final assault is concerned, have not been fully or correctly given in any of the current histories of Texas. The reason is obvious when it is remembered that not a single combatant from within survived to tell the tale, while the official reports of the enemy were neither circumstantial nor reliable. A trustworthy account of the assault could only be compiled by comparing and combining the verbal narratives of such of the assailants as could be relied on for veracity, and adding to this such light on the matter as may be gathered from military documents of that day. As Colonel Potter was a resident of Matamoros when the event happened, and for several months after the invading armies had returned thither, he had opportunities for obtaining the kind of information referred to which few persons, if any, still living in Texas have possessed ; and he has been urged to publish what he gathered on the subject, as by means of it an interesting fragment of history may be saved. He thus narrates his experience.

" Among the facts which have been perverted by both sides is the number of Mexican troops engaged in the assault and in the campaign. The whole force with which Santa Anna invaded Texas in 1836 probably amounted to about 7500 men. It consisted of two regiments of horse and thirteen battalions of foot. It may be well here to observe that the Mexicans apply the term regiment only to cavalry corps. Those of infantry of the same size are always called battalions ; and the latter term as used by them designates the whole of a colonel's command of foot, not as with us a subdivision of it. The nominal complement of a regiment or battalion is 1500 men ; but I have never known one to be full, or to much exceed a third of that number. It is seldom attempted to swell them beyond 500 men, for it is only by keeping down the strength, to keep up the number of the corps, that the numerous officers entitled to pay and clamorous for commands can be employed. I saw all the corps which returned from the campaign of '36, and from the size of those which had not been in action, as well as from the remaining bulk of those which had suffered, after allowing for probable loss, I am convinced that their average strength when they entered Texas differed little from 500—making the aggregate of the army as above surmised. That this estimate will apply to the third of it engaged in storming the Alamo I consider very probable, for I paid more attention to the strength of these corps than of others.

"At the beginning of the invasion the Mexican officers spoke of their army as 10,000 strong. After its failure Santa Anna, in his letter to General Jackson, referred to his invading force as having numbered 6000. This is the usual Mexican style of overrating, as a threat before action, and underrating, as an apology, after defeat. The truth is usually to be found midway between the two estimates.*

---

* When Santa Anna summoned General Taylor to surrender at Buena Vista, he announced his force as being over 20,000 strong. After his repulse he reported it to his Government as 16,000. 18,000 was probably near the truth.

"The main army, commanded by Santa Anna in person, moved from Laredo upon San Antonio in four successive detachments. This was rendered necessary by the scarcity of pasture and water in certain portions of the route. The lower division, commanded by Brigadier-General Urrea, moved from Matamoros upon Goliad in one body. It consisted of the cavalry regiment of Cuatla, the infantry battalion of Yucatan, and some companies of permanent militia. The aforesaid battalion, which I counted, numbered 350 odd men. The regiment of dragoons was of about the same size, and the whole made 900 or 1000.*

"The advance detachment from Laredo, consisting of the dragoon regiment of Dolores and one or two battalions, arrived at San Antonio in the latter part of February—I think on the 21st. The Alamo was at that time garrisoned by 156 men under Lieutenant-Colonel Travis. James Bowie was, I think, considered his second in command. David Crockett, of Tennessee, also belonged to this garrison, having joined it a few weeks before; but whether he had any command or not I have never heard. One of the most estimable and chivalrous men attached to it was J. B. Bonham, Esq., of South Carolina, who had recently come to volunteer in the service of Texas; but what his position was in the fortress I am unable to say. Travis had been commissioned by the Provisional Government of Texas a lieutenant-colonel of regular cavalry; but his corps had not been raised, and the men he now commanded were volunteers. Some of them had been engaged in the recent siege of San Antonio, when Cos capitulated, and others had more lately arrived from the United States. Among them were only

---

* This was the force, leaving out two small detachments, which overtook Fannin at Coleto; but it was reinforced before the surrender by two battalions from San Antonio, and by others a few days after.

three Mexicans of San Antonio, and what proportion the old residents of Texas bore to the newly arrived among them I am unable to say.

"No regular scouting service seems to have been kept up from Travis's post ; for, though the enemy was expected, his near approach was not known until his advance of dragoons was seen descending the slope west of the San Pedro. The guard in town is said to have retired in good order to the fort ; yet so complete was the surprise of the place that one or more American residents, engaged in mercantile business, fled to the Alamo, leaving their stores open. After the enemy entered the place, a cannon-shot from the Alamo was answered by a shell from the invaders ; and, I think, little more was done in the way of hostility that day. The fortress was not immediately invested, and the few citizens who had taken refuge in it succeeded in leaving it that night.

"On the 23rd, Santa Anna with the second division arrived,* and on the same day a regular siege was commenced. Its operations, which lasted eleven days, are, I think, correctly given in Yoakum's "History of Texas," though he did not succeed in getting a true account of the assault. Several batteries were opened on successive days, on the north, south, and east of the Alamo, where there were then no houses to interfere with the operations. The enemy, however, had no siege train, but only light field-pieces and howitzers. A breach was opened in the northern barrier, but the buildings seem not to have been severely battered. The operations of the siege consisted of an active though not very effective cannonade and bombardment, with occasional skirmishing by day, and frequent harassing alarms at night, designed to wear out the garrison by want of sleep. No

* Yoakum, in his "History of Texas," errs in supposing that the advance division arrived at San Antonio with Santa Anna on the 23rd. He was preceded by another, as here related.

assault was attempted, as has often been asserted, till the final storming of the place. Neither was the investment so close as to prevent the passage of couriers and the entrance of one small reinforcement; for, on the night of the 1st of March, a company of thirty-two men from Gonzales made its way through the enemy's lines, and entered the Alamo, never again to leave it. This raised the force of the garrison to 188 men, as none of the original number had yet fallen. There could have been no great loss on either side till the final assault.*

"Santa Anna, after calling a council of war on the 4th of March, fixed upon the morning of Sunday, the 6th, as the time for the final assault.

"It was resolved by Santa Anna that the assault should take place at early dawn. The order for the attack, which I have read, but have no copy of, was full and precise in its details, and was signed by Brigadier-General Amador as head of the staff. The besieging force consisted of the battalions of Toluca, Jimenes, Matamoros, los Zapadores (or sappers), and another, which I think was that of Guerrero, and the dragoon regiment of Dolores. The infantry were directed at a certain hour, between midnight and dawn, to form at a convenient distance from the port in four columns of attack and a reserve. This disposition was not made by battalions; for the light companies of all

---

* In a letter of Travis, dated March 3rd, he says: "With 145 men I have held this place ten days against a force variously estimated from 1500 to 6000; and I shall continue to hold it till I get relief from my countrymen, or I will perish in its defence. We have had a shower of bombs and cannon-balls continually falling among us the whole time; yet none of us have fallen. We have been miraculously preserved." Travis must have alluded to the original force of the garrison before the arrival of the Gonzales company. If its full number was 156, eleven men must have been non-effective from sickness or wounds, as none had been killed.

of them were incorporated with the Zapadores to form the reserve, and some other transpositions may have been made. A certain number of scaling ladders and axes were to be borne with particular columns. The cavalry were to be stationed at different points around the fortress to cut off fugitives. From what I have learned of men engaged in the action, it seems that these dispositions were changed on the eve of attack, so far as to combine the five bodies of infantry into three columns of atttck. This included the troops designated in the order as the reserve; and the only actual reserve that remained was the cavalry.

"The immediate command of the assault was entrusted to General Castrillon, a Spaniard by birth and a brilliant soldier. Santa Anna took his station, with a part of his staff and all the regimental bands, at a battery south of the Alamo and near the old bridge, from which the signal was to be given by a bugle note for the columns to move simultaneously at double quick time against different points of the fortress. One, composed mainly of the battalion of Toluca, was to enter the north breach; the other two to move against the southern side—one to attack the gate of the large area; the other to storm the chapel. By the timing of the signal it was calculated the columns would reach the foot of the wall just as it became light enough to operate.

"When the hour came the batteries and the music were alike silent, and a single blast of the bugle was at first followed by no sound save the rushing tramp of soldiers. The guns of the fortress soon opened upon them, and then the bands at the south battery struck up the assassin note of *dequello!* * But a few and not very effective discharges from the works could be made before the enemy was under them; † and it is thought

* No quarter.
† A sergeant of the Zapadores told me that the column he belonged to encountered but one discharge of grape in moving up, and that passed mostly over the men's heads.

that the worn and wearied garrison was not till then fully mustered. The Toluca column arrived first at the foot of the wall, but was not the first to enter the area. A large piece of cannon at the north-west angle of the area probably commanded the breach. Either this or the deadly fire of the riflemen at that point, where Travis commanded in person, brought the column to a disordered halt, and its leader, Colonel Duque, fell dangerously wounded. But, while this was occurring, one of the other columns entered the area by the gate or by escalade near it. The defence of the outer walls had now to be abandoned, and the garrison took refuge in the building already described. It was probably while the enemy were pouring in through the breach that Travis fell at his post, for his body was found beside the gun just referred to. All this passed within a few minutes after the bugle sounded. The early loss of the outer barrier, so thinly manned, was inevitable ; and it was not till the garrison became more concentrated and covered in the inner works, that the main struggle commenced. They were more concentrated as to the space, not as to unity ; for there was no communicating between buildings, nor in all cases between rooms. There was now no retreating from point to point ; and each group of defenders had to fight and die in the den where it was brought to bay. From the doors, windows, and loopholes of the several rooms around the area, the crack of the rifle and hiss of the bullet came fierce and fast : as fast the enemy fell and recoiled in his first efforts to charge. The gun beside which Travis lay was now turned against the buildings, as were also some others ; and shot after shot in quick succession was sent crashing through the doors and barricades of the several rooms. Each ball was followed by a storm of musketry and a charge ; and thus room after room was carried at the point of the bayonet, when all within them died fighting to the last. The struggle was made up of a number of separate and desperate combats, often hand to hand, between squads of the garrison and bodies of the enemy. The bloodiest spot about the fortress was the long barrack and the ground in front of it, where the enemy fell in heaps.

" In the mean time the turning of Travis's gun had been imitated by the garrison. A small piece on the roof of the chapel or one of the other buildings was turned against the area while the rooms were being stormed. It did more execution than any other cannon of the fortress ; but, after a few effective discharges, all who manned it fell under the enemy's fire. Crockett had taken refuge in a room of the low barrack near the gate. He either garrisoned it alone, or was left alone by the fall of his companions, when he sallied to meet his fate in the face of the foe, and was shot down. Bowie had been severely hurt by a fall from a platform, and, when the attack came on, was confined to his bed in an upper room of the barrack. He was there killed on his couch, but not without resistance ; for he is said to have shot down with his pistols one or more of the enemy as they entered the chamber.

" The church was the last point taken. The column which moved against it, consisting of the battalion of Jimenes and other troops, was at first repulsed, and took refuge among some old houses outside of the barrier, near its south-west angle, till it was rallied and led on by General Amador. It was soon joined by the rest of the force, and the church was carried by a *coup de main.* Its inmates, like the rest, fought till the last, and continued to fire from the upper platforms after the enemy occupied the floor of the building. A Mexican officer told of seeing a man shot in the crown of the head in this *mêlée.* During the closing struggle Lieutenant Dickenson, with his child in his arms, or tied to his back, as some accounts say, leaped from an upper window, and both were killed in the act. Of those he left behind him the bayonet soon gleaned what the bullet missed ; and in the upper part of the church the last defender must have fallen. The morning breeze which received his parting breath probably still fanned his flag above that fabric ere it was pulled down by the victors.*

"*The Alamo had fallen.*

"The action, according to Santa Anna's report, lasted thirty minutes. It was certainly short ; and possibly no longer space passed between the moment the enemy fronted the breach and that when resistance died out. Some of the incidents which have to be related separately no doubt occurred simultaneously, and occupied very little time.

"The account of the assault which Yoakum and others have adopted as authentic, is evidently one which popular tradition has based on conjecture. By a rather natural inference it assumes that the enclosing wall of the fortress was its principal work, that in storming this the main conflict took place, and that after it was entered nothing more than the death struggles of a few occurred. The truth was, that extensive barrier proved to be nothing more than the outworks, speedily lost, while the buildings constituted the citadel and the scene of the sternest resistance. That Santa Anna himself was under the works, urging on the escalade in person, is exceedingly fabulous.

"A negro boy belonging to Travis, the wife of Lieutenant Dickenson, Mrs. Alsbury (a native of St. Antonio) and another Mexican woman, and two children, were the only inmates of the fortress whose lives were spared. The children were those of the two females whose names

---

* It is a fact not often remembered, that Travis and his men died under the Mexican Federal flag of 1824, instead of the "Lone Star," although the Independence of Texas, unknown to them, had been declared four days before. They died for a republic whose existence they never knew.

are given.   Lieutenant Dickenson commanded a gun in the east upper window of the church.   His family was probably in one of the two small upper rooms of the front.   This will account for his being able to take one of his children to the rear platform while the building was being stormed.   A small irrigating canal runs below the window referred to ; and his aim, in the desperate attempt at flight, probably was to break his fall by leaping into the water ; but the shower of bullets which greeted him rendered the precaution as needless as it was hopeless.

"About the time the outer barriers were carried, a few men leaped from them and attempted to escape, but were all cut down by the cavalry.   Half an hour or more after the action was over a few men were found concealed in one of the rooms under some mattresses; General Houston, in a letter of the 11th, says as many as seven ; but I have generally heard them spoken of as only three or four.   The officer to whom they were first reported entreated Santa Anna to spare their lives ; but he was sternly rebuked and the men ordered to be shot, which was done.   Owing to the hurried and confused manner in which the mandate was obeyed, a Mexican soldier was accidentally killed with them.

"Castrillon was the soul of the assault.   Santa Anna remained at the south battery, with the music of the whole army and a part of his staff, till he supposed the place was nearly mastered, when he moved up with that escort towards the Alamo ; but returned again on being greeted by a few rifle-balls from the upper windows of the church.   He, however, entered the area towards the close of the scene, and directed some of the last details of the butchery.

"The five infantry corps that formed the attacking force, according to the data already referred to, amounted to about 2500 men.   The number of Mexican wounded, according to various accounts, largely exceeded that of

the killed ; and the estimates made of both by intelligent men who were in the action, and whose candour,
I think, could be relied on, rated their loss at from
150 to 200 killed, and from 300 to 400 wounded.
Santa Anna's report is a piece of balderdash dealing
mostly in generalities. He sets down his force at 1400,
his loss at 60 killed and 300 wounded, and the strength
of the garrison, all told and all killed, at 600. This
is about as reliable as the legend of old Texans, that
the Alamo was stormed by 10,000 men, 1000 of whom
were slain. The real loss of the assailants in killed
and wounded probably did not differ much from 500
men. General Bradburn was of opinion that 300
men in that action were lost to the service, counting
with the killed those who died of wounds or were per-
manently disabled. This agrees with the other most
reliable estimates.* Now, if 500 men or more were
bullet-stricken in half an hour by 180 or less, it was a
rapidity of bloodshed almost unexampled, and needs no
exaggeration. It was not the carnage of pursuit like

---

* Anselmo Borgara, a Mexican, who first reported the fall of the
Alamo to General Houston at Gonzales, and who left San Antonio
on the evening after it occurred, stated that the assaulting force
amounted to about 2300 men, of whom 521 were killed and as
many wounded. He had probably either had opportunities of seeing and estimating the bulk of the besieging force, or had his
information on this point from those who had a tolerably correct
idea of its strength. It probably did not exceed 2500 men, nor
much fall below that number. The loss, however, is evidently
exaggerated, because it is simply incredible. We would have to
search history closely to find where any troops have carried a fortress with a loss of more than two-fifths of that number. If there
was any basis for this part of the statement, it is probable that 521
was the entire loss of killed and wounded, which at second-hand
would become that of killed alone, and then it would be assumed
that the number of wounded was equal. General Houston seems to
have gathered from this man the idea that Travis had only 150
effective men out of 187.—(Letter of March 11th to Fannia.) But
if none had fallen up to the 3rd, the effective force could hardly
have been reduced so much in the next two days and nights.

that of San Jacinto, nor the sweeping effect of cannon under favourable circumstances like that of Sandusky. The main element of the defence was the individual valour and skill of men who had few advantages of fortification, ordnance, discipline, or command. All their deficiencies, which were glaring, serve only to enhance the one merit, in which no veterans could have excelled them. It required bravery even in greatly superior numbers to overcome a resistance so determined. The Mexican troops displayed more of it in this assault than in any other action during the campaign ; and they have seldom shown as much anywhere.

"Santa Anna, when he marched for Texas, had counted on finding a fortified position in the neighbourhood of San Antonio, but not at the Alamo ; for he supposed, with good reason, that the Mission of Concepcion would be selected. The small area of that strong building, which had room enough for Travis's force and not too much, and its compactness, which would have given better range to his cannon, would have made it a far better fortress than the Alamo ; and earthworks of no great extent would have covered the garrison's access to the river. The advantages of the position must have been known to Travis, and that he did not avail himself of it was probably owing to his imperfect command of men unwilling to leave their town associations. An attempt to move might break up the garrison. The neglect of scouting service, before referred to, indicates a great lack of subordination, for Travis, who during the late siege of Bexar had been the efficient head of that branch of duty, must have been aware of its importance. On the 24th of February he wrote thus : ' When the enemy appeared in sight we had not three bushels of corn. We have since found in deserted houses eighty or ninety bushels, and got into the walls twenty or thirty head of beeves.' This omission to provide, remedied so late by accident, must have been more owing to the commander's lack of control and to the occupation of mind incident to it, than to his want of foresight. His men were willing to die by him, but, I infer, not ready to obey in what did not immediately concern fighting.

"I am here tempted to speculate briefly on the bearing which it might have had on the campaign, had Travis changed his post to the Mission, strengthened it to the best of his ability, and secured a supply of provisions for a few weeks. The great importance Santa Anna attached to an early blow and rapid movement would probably have induced him to make an assault there as early, or nearly so, as he did at the Alamo; and there, even had his force been stronger, I am confident the result would have been different. Instead of the panic which the fall of the Alamo spread through the land, sending fugitives to the Sabine, a bloody repulse from Concepcion would have filled Texas with exultation, and sent its men in crowds to Houston's camp. The fortress could then have held out till relieved; and the war would probably have been finished west of the Guadalupe. Its final results could not have been more disastrous to the invaders than they eventually were; but a large extent of country would have been saved from invasion and partial devastation.

"A military lesson may be derived from the fall of the Alamo. Among the essential qualities of a perfect soldier we must consider, not only the discipline and subordination which blend him with the mass in which the word of command moves him, but also the individual self-reliance and efficiency which may restore the battle after the mass is broken. From the lack of the former quality the men of the Alamo were lost; by their possession of the latter they became, in the last struggle, as formidable as veterans and died gloriously, and in a better position they would have been saved by it. Though the latter quality depends more on nature

R

than the former, it admits of development, and the perfection of training neglects neither.

"Of the foregoing details which do not refer to documentary authority I obtained many from General Bradburn, who arrived at San Antonio a few days after the action, and gathered them from officers who were in it. A few I had through a friend from General Amador. Others, again, I received from three intelligent sergeants, who were men of fair education and, I think, truthful. One of them, Sergeant Becero, of the battalion of Matamoros, who was captured at San Jacinto, was for several years my servant in Texas. From men of their class I could generally get more candid statements as to loss and other matters than from commissioned officers. I have also gathered some minor particulars from local tradition preserved among the residents of this town. When most of the details thus learned were acquired I had not seen the locality ; and hence I have to locate some of the occurrences by inference, which I have done carefully and, I think, correctly.

"The stranger will naturally inquire, 'Where lie the heroes of the Alamo ?' and Texas can only reply by a silent blush. A few hours after the action, the bodies of the slaughtered garrison were gathered up by the victors, laid in three piles, mingled with fuel, and burned.* On the 25th of February, near a year after, their bones and ashes were collected, placed in a coffin, and interred with due solemnity, and with military honours, by Colonel Seguin and his command. The place of burial was in what was then a peach orchard outside the town and a few hundred yards from the Alamo. It is now a large enclosed lot in the midst of the Alamo suburb, but has fortunately not been built upon. The rude landmarks which once designated the

---

* Their own dead were carted across the San Pedro and buried.

place of burial have long since disappeared, and it would now require diligent search to find the exact locality. It is to be hoped that search will not be delayed till it is too late.

"The Government of the State of Texas has never secured or preserved but one memento of the Alamo. A small but finely executed monument was made from the stones of the fortress in 1841 by an artist named Nangle ; and, after lying long neglected, it was purchased by the State. It now stands in the hall of the Capitol at Austin ; but neither at the Alamo itself, nor at the forgotten grave of its defenders, does any legend or device, like the stone of Thermopylæ, remind the stranger of those who died for their country's rights."

THE END.

PRINTED AT THE CAXTON PRESS, BECCLES.

BOOKS FOR YOUNG READERS,
Continued.

TWO FRIENDS. By LUCIAN BIART, Author of "The
Adventures of a Young Naturalist," "My Rambles in the New World,"
&c. Translated by MARY DE HAUTEVILLE. Small post 8vo., numerous
Illustrations, price 7s. 6d.

"Extremely interesting. Boys cannot fail to be delighted with it. . . . Is
beautifully got up."—*Scotsman.*

MR. W. H. G. KINGSTON'S NEW BOYS' BOOK IS

WITH AXE AND RIFLE ON THE WESTERN
PRAIRIES. By W. H. G. KINGSTON. Fully Illustrated, cloth gilt,
price 7s. 6d.

"The reader will find in this book that which pleases every boy."—*Scotsman.*

THE CURIOUS ADVENTURES OF A FIELD
CRICKET. By Dr. ERNEST CANDEZE. Translated by N. D'ANVERS.
Fully Illustrated. Crown 8vo, cloth extra, gilt edges, price 7s. 6d.

"Simply charming. The story runs trippingly, and is highly humorous.
. . . The Illustrations are as amusing as the text."—*Scotsman.*

MY RAMBLES IN THE NEW WORLD. Translated
by MARY DE HAUTEVILLE. Fully Illustrated. Cloth extra, large post
8vo, 7s. 6d.

"Full of stories of marvellous adventures; the illustrations are excellent;
the work is one that boys may well prize. The translation appears to have
been excellently done."—*Scotsman.*

THE LITTLE KING; or, The Taming of a Young Russian
Count. By S. BLANDY. 64 Illustrations. Crown 8vo, cloth extra, gilt,
7s. 6d.

"There is a great deal worth reading in this book."—*Pall Mall Gazette.*

"A very pleasant and interesting volume, which we would recommend to
our readers."—*Spectator.*

"Excellently translated."—*Athenæum.*

HANS BRINKER; or, The Silver Skates. By Mrs. M.
DODGE. An entirely New Edition, with 59 full-page and other Woodcuts.
Square crown 8vo, cloth extra, 7s. 6d.; Text only, paper, 1s.

MY BROTHER JACK; or, The Story of What-d'ye-call-'em.
Written by himself. By ALPHONSE DAUDET. Illustrated. Square 16mo,
cloth, 7s. 6d.

"MY KALULU," PRINCE, KING, AND SLAVE. A Story
from Central Africa. By HENRY M. STANLEY, the Great Traveller.
Illustrated. Cloth, 7s. 6d.

SAMPSON LOW, MARSTON, SEARLE & RIVINGTON,
CROWN BUILDINGS, 188, FLEET STREET, E.C.